PUFFIN

The Hairy Hands

Gene Kemp grew up near Tamworth in the Midlands, took a degree at Exeter University, taught, married and had three children. She is best known for her Cricklepit School stories, which include *The Turbulent Term of Tyke Tiler* (winner of the Carnegie Medal and the Other Award), *Gowie Corby Plays Chicken*, *Charlie Lewis Plays for Time* (runner-up for the Whitbread Award 1985) and *Just Ferret* (runner-up for the Smarties Award in 1990). In addition are *The Clock Tower Ghost*, *Jason Bodger and the Priory Ghost*, *Juniper*, short stories, a poetry anthology, and writings for TV and radio. In 1984 Gene Kemp was awarded an honorary degree for her books, which have been translated into numerous languages.

Gene Kemp lives in Exeter. Her hobbies include taking an interest in wildlife, reading as much as possible, watching TV, exploring Dartmoor, supporting Aston Villa and Exeter, playing with her grandchildren and doing nothing.

Some other books by Gene Kemp

THE CLOCK TOWER GHOST
JASON BODGER AND THE PRIORY GHOST
THE PUFFIN BOOK OF GHOSTS AND GHOULS
(Ed.)

The Cricklepit series in reading order:

THE TURBULENT TERM OF TYKE TILER
GOWIE CORBY PLAYS CHICKEN
CHARLIE LEWIS PLAYS FOR TIME
JUST FERRET
ZOWEY CORBY AND THE BLACK CAT TUNNEL

Gene Kemp

The Hairy Hands

Illustrated by Peter Viccars

PUFFIN BOOKS

PUFFIN BOOKS

Published by the Penguin Group
Penguin Books Ltd, 27 Wrights Lane, London W8 5TZ, England
Penguin Putnam Inc., 375 Hudson Street, New York, New York 10014, USA
Penguin Books Australia Ltd, Ringwood, Victoria, Australia
Penguin Books Canada Ltd, 10 Alcorn Avenue, Toronto, Ontario, Canada M4V 3B2
Penguin Books (NZ) Ltd, Private Bag 102902, NSMC, Auckland, New Zealand

Penguin Books Ltd, Registered Offices: Harmondsworth, Middlesex, England

First published 1999
4

Text copyright © Gene Kemp, 1999
Illustrations copyright © Peter Viccars, 1999
All rights reserved

The acknowledgements on page 133 constitute an extension of this copyright page

The moral right of the author and illustrator has been asserted

Set in 13/14.5 pt Monotype Ehrhardt
Typeset by Rowland Phototypesetting Ltd,
Bury St Edmunds, Suffolk
Made and printed in England by Clays Ltd, St Ives plc

British Library Cataloguing in Publication Data
A CIP catalogue record for this book is available from the British Library

ISBN 0–141–30278–X

1721

Dark night on Dartmoor.

Suddenly the clouds break in their wind-blown scurry across the sky and the moon shines out. The lonely road over the bleak moorlands is as white and clear as if it were day. A man on horseback whips and pushes his steed to a gallop, for the moor is no place to be late at night.

This stretch of road has an especially evil reputation: people have died here. Eating and drinking and laughing with his friends, the rider never gave the journey home a thought. He wasn't afraid then, but *now* he is full of fear.

He glances quickly behind him, urges his horse, faster, faster. Soon he'll be at the Warren House Inn in the middle of the moor. There he'll feel safe. The moon sails across the sky and raggedy clouds stream past it, blown by the wind, for the night is wild. The horseman longs for the safety of home with his wife and children, totally forgotten while he was drinking earlier.

He looks behind him again. Sees nothing, only the night and the moor. A faint light gleams out from the old powder mills in the distance and it cheers him.

He feels he's not alone after all and so he slows down a little, for his horse is hot, tiring, and so is he. He takes a deep breath. He's almost home. Almost safe.

A pair of huge, muscular hands sprinkled with black hairs closes over his.

'No!' he screams. The horse neighs and rears high in the air, as terrified as its rider. Both try to struggle free.

But the hands are much stronger. The horse's knees buckle as clouds cover the sky and the road darkens as the rider flies over his horse's head.

Terrified, the animal breaks loose and bolts across the moor.

Much later next day the horse is found, calmed and captured. By this time, its owner too has been discovered, dead on that moorland road with his neck broken.

1821

On a damp night in March, Edith Hunter and her beau, Wilfred Edwards, are travelling across the moor in a horse-drawn carriage for their regular evening playing cards. As they approach a bridge high above a river valley, they are engaged in conversation and neither is aware of what happens next.

Their driver is, though, when a pair of hairy hands suddenly seizes the reins, throwing him from his seat. The horses rear up madly and shoot away, breaking free from their harness. The carriage spins out of control and shoots down a gully, ending up smashed to pieces in the bottom of the river. The lovers are found dead in each other's arms.

But the driver escapes, miraculously unscathed, and on many later occasions is to be found at the same spot. Edith Hunter had been a wealthy lady, and several pieces of jewellery, including a pearl necklace, are lying somewhere in the river, which is why he is to be found painstakingly searching for them. We don't know whether or not he is ever successful.

June 1921

A doctor rides a motorbike along the road from Postbridge to Princetown. It's early morning and he's been called out to Dartmoor prison on an emergency. His wife is at home with a new baby, and he takes the older boy and girl in the motorbike's sidecar so she can rest.

Suddenly he yells, 'Jump! There's something wrong!'

The bike swerves crazily, the engine breaks loose, the doctor flies over the handlebars and is killed.

But the children roll out and are saved.

August 1921

A young army officer leaves a friend's house on his motorbike, cheerily waving goodbye.

Much later he crawls back cut, bruised, trembling, his bike left behind, a write-off.

'What happened?' asks his friend, tending his injuries.

The young man can only moan and gasp, 'The hands! The hairy hands!'

Chapter One

Tom Fraser flung open the door, threw his school bag at the bottom of the stairs and kicked the skirting-board as hard as he could several times.

He was wearing plimsolls and his howls of rage and pain brought his sister Jessica out of the kitchen, where she was making a peanut butter sandwich. Some of the peanut butter dropped on the floor. Unhurriedly, she scooped it up and licked it lovingly off her finger. She finished her sandwich, then: 'What's up?' she asked.

Tom lay crashed out, banging his head quite gently every now and then on the floor.

'One of these days you'll break something doing that,' she murmured. 'D'you want a peanut butter sandwich? I'm having some more.'

Tom didn't answer. Just lay there moaning and banging and kicking until Jessica went back to the kitchen and returned, surprisingly quickly, with two sandwiches and two drinks. At last Tom sat up and took a sandwich. They ate sitting on the hall floor.

Tom is skinny and dark and fierce and quick. Jessica's big and fair with one fat, golden plait down her back. They're not alike. Tom's a volcano exploding. Jessica's so laid-back she's practically horizontal. Their mother died long enough ago for them not to be sad about it any more. But they say 'Hi' every morning to her picture on the landing, painted by their father, Andrew Fraser.

'Tell me,' she said.

'I hate him, I hate him, I hate him,' Tom replied.

'No, don't start banging yourself again. You'll do yourself an injury – to say nothing of the skirting. Dad only painted it *again* last week and he'll go ballistic. Just tell me what's up.'

'Him. Him. Him. That new kid.'

'Who's he when he's at school?'

'The one who came this term. And old Barker's given him my place in the team . . . ! My place. What I've worked for . . .'

Tom almost howled in sorrow and despair.

'. . . and old Barker – he likes him, the pig – he promised it to me last term, I thought.'

His face crumpled up. Tears shot everywhere. No one could cry like Tom. All his body and soul went into it. Jessica leaned over and wiped his tears with her plait. She'd been doing it for years. She never cried.

'Can't you play somewhere else in the team?'

'No, I'm a striker. I don't play anywhere else!!!'

'How many are there?'

'Two. And Alan Sherman's the other one and he's team captain so he's got to be there. But I was gonna be the other one. And now it's him, this new kid.'

'But why can't you play somewhere else?'

'Because I'm no good in defence or midfield. I've told you over and over again about the team. You don't listen.'

'No,' agreed Jessica, licking her fingers. 'It's a bit boring. Want another slice?'

'No, I don't.'

'Well, I'll just get some of the new orange chocolate biscuits. Mrs Murdoch's hidden 'em but I know where they are. Want one?'

'Oh, I don't care. I feel like KILLING MYSELF!'

'Well, have a chocky bic first,' Jessica said. 'Before you die. It'll give you strength to kill yourself.'

'He's stolen my place,' mumbled Tom, spluttering out chocolate bits.

'It's unfair of old Barker,' murmured Jessica soothingly.

'But he's better than me. He's faster and he's brilliant. Like lightning. And his finishes! Goal after goal. He's gonna be great. Like George Best.'

'That's nice,' Jessica said, on her third biscuit.

'But I wanted it to be me!'

'Tough. What's he called, this wizard genius?'

'Felix.'

'Cor. Fancy, eh?'

She wiped some crumbs off her plait.

'You're not left out altogether?'

'No, I'm first sub.'

'Right. Well, I'll see if I can find someone at school to trip Alan Sherman or this new kid up and then break their ankles.'

'You can't do that! We can't do anything.'

'No. But never mind, Tom. Something will happen.'

'No, it won't. It never has. Life goes on just the same. Dad and Mrs Murdoch at home and me always on the sub's bench at school. I was there all last year and now just when I thought I'd made it – there I am again.'

'Something will happen . . .'

The door opened.

'Hello, Dad!'

'Hello, kids. What a mess! Clean it up.'

No one moved.

'Oh, come on. Please. Don't leave it all to me.'

'OK, I'll do it,' Jessica said. 'Tom's in a mood.'

'He's always in a mood,' sighed their father.

Chapter Two

The Frasers led a peaceful life even though Tom exploded now and then. Mrs Murdoch came in to help out, Dad drove his taxi – he'd given up teaching two years ago (too much stress, he said), so he would have more spare time to get on with his painting. Not that he did, he just spent more and more time driving all over the place for people and just thinking about painting. Jessica read loads of magazines, listened to pop music and thought about food. Tom practised and practised his football skills and didn't quite make the team.

But one day their father brought the Pattersons home for the first time, and the Fraser world whizzed round and turned upside down and inside out, never to be the same again.

'Jessica,' he appealed (no use appealing to Tom) from where he stood, looking worried stiff, hair standing up in squiffs, specs skew-whiffed, old crumply cords, old crumply face, a cosy man, Andrew Fraser. 'Jessica . . . and Tom . . . come and meet Clem and her boys.'

Jessica could tell he was very nervous. Behind her she knew that Tom was shuffling his size ten trainers, breathing hard, about to explode, his hot anger hitting her in the back of the neck.

Silence hung in the room.

'Jessica,' repeated her father, meaning help me, help me, help me out, you always do, you're always on my side. Please. 'Come and meet Clem and Felix and Jack. I hope you'll be friends.'

And that's when Jessica somehow knew. Even before Tom shouted, 'What's HE doing here? In our house?' she realized that (a) Dad had got a new girlfriend at last and it might be serious, and (b) this Felix must be Tom's enemy, the wizard genius at football, Felix.

She didn't say anything, just stood there smiling a wide smiley smile at Clem who was also smiling a wide smiley smile at her. Her father just stood in the middle waving his hands, looking and sounding lost and silly.

'Jessica – Clem. Clem – Jessica.'

He looked at her appealingly. He counted on her support. He believed she always was on his side and so she was, except when it clashed with Tom. But she liked to keep the peace because it made things comfortable. Jessica liked things to be comfortable.

'Hello, Jessica,' smiled Clem, in a voice like a singer's. She was tall, taller than their father. And very beautiful. Like a model, a supermodel. She was also black. So were her boys.

'This is Felix,' she said, pulling him forward. He tried to pull back, face like thunder.

And Tom went ballistic.

'Get out!' he yelled. 'Get out of here!'

'Tom,' shouted his father. 'Tom, this is your new family.'

(Happy Families was off to a fine start.)

'I don't WANT a new family,' bellowed Tom. 'I need a new family like I need a hole in the head. I don't WANT a black family. And I don't WANT him – he's stolen my place in the team!'

'That's because I'm better than you,' sneered Felix. 'And if you don't want a black family I don't want a white one. So *there*.'

'Get out,' yelled Tom. 'Push off. Go!'

'You go,' his father shouted. 'Up to your room.'

Face white, Tom rushed out of the room and ran upstairs as Felix headed for the front door.

Standing struck dumb as her father muttered apologies to Clem, Jessica felt a hand push into hers. She looked down at him – Jack, was he called? – a funny little lad. Was there something wrong with his foot? He limped, she thought. His face was thin, his eyes very big, and then he grinned, a terrific grin that changed his look completely, a wicked, mischievous grin.

'I like *you*, Jessica,' he said. 'Don't take any notice of them.'

She didn't know what to say. But after a minute she grinned back and said, 'Come into the kitchen and we'll have a peanut butter sandwich.'

Chapter Three

'Now tell me all about it, Dad,' Jessica murmured later that evening as she cooked cheese on toast for supper. Sounds of banging came from above their heads, where Tom was either practising football skills in his bedroom or taking out his rage on the furniture. They were used to both and took no notice.

Once started, her father poured out the story as if he'd turned on a bath tap. He hadn't enjoyed keeping secrets from Jessica and he wanted to tell her all about the new wonder and excitement coming into all their lives. Now since she'd been about seven, Jessica had privately always thought she was somehow older and had more sense than her dad, to say nothing of Tom, so she listened patiently.

'How did you meet her – Clem?'

'She was late coming home from work one

night. It was raining, her car had broken down and she'd missed the bus so she took my taxi. She was very worried about being late for the babysitter and she started to talk non-stop. I felt sorry for her. She told me about her little boy Jack having to have lots of operations for his foot and said her other boy Felix was great, but did get stroppy.'

'Don't I know it,' Andrew had said. 'I've got a boy like that – his name's Tom. He's OK if he gets his own way but if he doesn't all hell's let loose.'

'How old is he?"

He told her.

'Why, that's the same age as Felix.'

'Tom's crazy about football . . .'

'SNAP! So's Felix . . .'

'And he's good. In the school team. Well, he's first sub.'

'SNAP! So's Felix, in the school team.'

They were laughing by then, and Clem told Andrew all about Jack and the treatment he'd had to have, and her training to be a nurse after being a model, and how brave Jack had been through all the operations and everything, but that one day her husband said enough was enough, she'd changed, and now home was just a bloomin' orthopaedic ward and he was off, out of it. They never saw him again.

She had cried then. On his shoulder. (Andrew

was sitting in the back of the cab by this time.) Jessica knew her dad was easy to cry on. Comfy. Sympathetic.

'We sat quiet for a bit,' Andrew said. 'Then I told her about you, Jessica. That you were like machine oil that makes everything work properly . . .'

'Look, I'm not a car, Dad! I'm not *oil*. Sounds horrible. Ugh.'

'You know what I mean, Jessica. *She* knew. She said you sounded nice and she wished she'd got a daughter . . .'

'Did she ask about Mum?'

He sat quiet for a bit, then: 'Yes. And I told her about Mum dying of leukaemia and Gran, my mother, looking after us when you were little but now she'd gone back up north to be with her sister who was ill . . .'

'It must have been an expensive taxi ride with you two rabbiting on for ages, Dad.'

'I didn't even notice. Then she asked me in and I had coffee with her and met the kids, and I got to know them. Jack's terrific. And Felix – he's just like Tom.'

'I noticed. Horrible.'

They both sighed.

'You don't mind, do you, Jessica? It's not that I don't love you and Tom. But I do love Clem and she loves me, and we want to get married.'

'Dad, I don't mind you getting married again.

You ought to, and she seems OK. I like her. I'm not *jealous* or anything. It's just that . . .'

'Just what . . . ?'

'It's not easy, is it?'

'Why not? Why shouldn't I get married? What business is it of anybody else? Oh, I don't mean that. Of course it's *your* business.'

'Oh, Dad.'

'I know, I know.'

'There's the neighbours,' said Jessica, desperately searching for reasons.

'We've got to lead our lives, not theirs.'

'Tom? Felix?'

'They'll get on once they start playing soccer together. And you and Clem'll get on fine. You need a mother, just getting into your teens. Jack'll love you, you'll see.'

'Do I need a *black* mother, Dad?' There. She'd said it. The unsayable, the unspeakable.

'Oh, Jessica. I'm counting on you. I do love her so. She's so beautiful. And so lovely. Please help me.'

'OK, OK. I'll try. I'll try.'

But she knew it wouldn't be easy.

It wasn't.

Chapter Four

At first Tom and Felix wouldn't even stay together in the same room without going for one another, while Andrew and Clem, in some kind of cloud-cuckoo-land, thought Jessica, talked about where they would all live. At his house – preferably – lots of garden there where the boys could practise football.

'Must be crazy,' Jessica said to Tom, who shouted, 'No way. That git's not coming here. NOT ON MY PATCH!'

Clem said it would be best to start off in a house new to all of them. But she'd only just moved!

'Expensive,' Andrew said. 'Moving's expensive.'

'I'd have to move with the boys anyway,' said Clem. 'So what's the difference for us?'

On and on they talked about it. Talking in circles getting nowhere, thought Jessica.

*

During the next week Tom threw a pizza at Felix and Felix broke a window at the Frasers' house. Jack had to go with Clem into hospital one night for observation so Felix came to sleep with them, and he and Tom both got up in the middle of the night to raid the fridge. Tom tried to shove Felix's head inside, and Jessica, woken up by the noise, got up and there they were punching each other, rolling over and over on the floor, ice-cubes and frozen food all over the place, Felix's nose bleeding, an egg-lump standing up on Tom's forehead.

The next row was over Jessica.

'She needs new clothes. She's got nothing!' cried Clem, who always looked like a model, even on nursing duty.

'She's got school uniform. And some jeans. What more does she want? Clothes cost money,' said her father.

'Huh,' sighed Clem. 'Men! Money! I hope you're not gonna turn out to be mean! I'll treat Jessica.'

One free Saturday they went to town and bought clothes Jessica hadn't even known existed, wow! Actually, her father was pleased when he saw her in them and said he hadn't realized. Clem tried to get him to buy some new ones as well, but that was a waste of time.

Tom wasn't shouting any more. He and Felix just didn't speak.

Andrew and Clem still hadn't decided when they were going to be married or where they were all going to live when the worst row occurred. It had to be about Jack. It just had to be.

Tom didn't shout at Felix any more but he still muttered things about him and Jack.

'Who's that kid in the Scrooge story, Jess? Tiny Tim or something. Well, *he's* today's version, I reckon. Didn't Tiny Tim die?' he added hopefully.

'You, Tom Fraser, are just the meanest, lowest form of life on this planet,' his sister replied. 'And don't you dare be horrible to him while I'm around or . . .'

'Or what?'

Jessica didn't answer *that*.

'I don't like Felix much but Jack's a great little kid. He's funny. He makes me laugh.'

'He makes me laugh too,' her brother replied. 'Especially when he tries to play football. Huh. Yuck.'

'The whole world isn't ruled by how people play football.'

'It's silly he even tries. He's spastic.'

'You're disgusting!' cried his father, coming in just then. 'Don't let me ever hear you say that word again. And just you take care how you treat him, d'you hear? He's a saint, that boy.'

'Yuck. Yuck. Yuck,' shouted Tom.

But one day after Jack had been fretful with his painful leg and Clem worried and fussing, Andrew came out with, 'You spoil him. You need to toughen him up so he can cope with life.'

'Needs putting down, you mean,' whispered Tom.

Everyone heard. Jack sat frozen, eyes enormous, silent, then limped over to his mother and put his head in her lap.

'Tom!' roared Andrew, incandescent with rage. 'Get upstairs and don't bother to come down tonight!'

'I'll kill him!' cried Felix, jumping like a firecracker. 'Let me get at him! He'll suffer.'

'You sit down and shut up as well!' shouted Andrew.

Clem said nothing. Very quietly, her face sculptured stone, she gathered her things together and took Jack by the hand.

'Don't go! He doesn't mean it!' Jessica cried. 'Clem, don't go.'

Clem walked out of the house holding Jack's hand, Felix behind them.

Andrew went to follow. Jessica stopped him.

'It's no good, Dad. Not now. Ring her up later.'

But she didn't answer the phone when Andrew rang, and when he went to the flat no one was there. Tom said that Felix wasn't at school. Andrew was broken-hearted.

It was a terrible time. Once Jessica found her dad crying. She kept worrying about him, and about Jack as well and was he OK? She realized how fond of him she'd grown.

One day he'd shown her his poor foot and she'd massaged it for him – and after that he always asked her to look at it and see if it was improved. Privately she thought she could have taken better care of the foot and of Jack himself than Clem did. But then Jessica was used to looking after people.

Tom was as happy as a mudlark, singing and shouting through the house, especially when he scored a hat-trick in a school football match.

It was hopeless, Jessica thought. Dad happy? Tom happy? You could have one or the other but not both.

Chapter Five

Tom leapt around humming and whistling and grinning, but his father moped,
squiffy hair sad and droopy, dark bags
under his eyes so he looked like a giant panda.

Mrs Murdoch told them she was leaving –
she was sorry but her husband had retired and
they were going to move, to live in the country
near her daughter. Sadly they said goodbye.
She'd been with them for ages.

Everything's changing, Jessica thought as
she struggled with the vacuum cleaner after
school.

'Can we get someone else to help, Dad?' she
pleaded, and he said OK, but it was clear he
wasn't actually going to do anything about it.
All he seemed interested in was the painting of
Clem he'd been working on. He would sit and
look at *that* for hours.

'Kick him,' Tom suggested when Jessica

complained. 'Hit him with your plait. That hurts.'

Jessica cooked some omelettes instead, wondering why everything had changed so suddenly.

'I don't like this,' she muttered. 'I don't like everything changing. Makes me nervous. I wish, I wish . . . things would change back again to make everyone happy.'

In the meantime, she settled for two bananas, a chocolate biscuit and a book in her bedroom.

Were Jessica's wishes granted? You never can tell with wishes. But next day Andrew's brother Peter rang up. He had recently returned from Australia and had taken a cottage on Dartmoor.

'What on earth will you do there?' Andrew asked.

He'd already formed a band, and had contacts with a travelling theatre company and Dartmoor prison, among others, Pete said.

'That'll suit you,' said his brother.

Pete was a musician, a wanderer, something of a traveller, always ready to move on, always enjoying life. He'd never married or settled down. Andrew had been the steady one, going to college, taking up teaching – only to give it up later in favour of painting and taxi-driving.

Pete invited them to stay for the half-term holiday.

'Oh, yes, please,' said Jessica.

'Great,' Tom agreed. He wanted to get away from school and even he couldn't fall out with Uncle Peter. Pete was one of the world's optimists – life was always sure to get better and one day they'd all be rich and happy.

Next day, walking down the High Street, Jessica met Clem and Jack by chance. Jack flung his arms round her and hugged her as if he never wanted to let go. Then she was hugged by Clem too.

They walked back together. Andrew opened the door and his face! Tequila Sunrise.

But when Tom came home and found them there *he* stormed out of the house and didn't return for hours. When he did come back in at last, very late, Jessica and his father were waiting up for him. Jessica was scared stiff, trying to stop Andrew blowing up at him, making everything worse than ever, but even as he came through the door Tom was talking like crazy.

'Can't we just go on as we are? You can see HER and I don't have to see THEM. That would do, wouldn't it? That would be all right?'

But Andrew Fraser wasn't having any.

'No,' he answered. 'I'm going to marry Clem and so you'll just have to put up with Felix and Jack.'

'I think you're mad!'

'Don't you dare speak like that to your father . . .'

'Oh, Dad, no! Please,' Jessica butted in.

'I just can't bear to think that my son's a racist. Not after the way you've been brought up.'

'I'm not a racist!' shouted Tom. 'There's black kids in my class and they're great and I like them but HIM, I'd never like *him* in a hundred years. He's horrible, bossy, a show-off, a stuck-up . . .'

'THAT'S ENOUGH!'

'. . . and I don't like the little one either.'

'And Clem, may I ask? What fault do you find with her?'

'Don't answer, Tom,' Jessica put in, caught between them as usual.

'Well, she's all right, I suppose. But she's not my mother, is she? That's my mother, there . . .'

He pointed to the picture on the landing, then ran half-way up the stairs and stood beside it, turning to shout . . .

'. . . and Clem will never ever be my mother!' Jessica could see the tears on his face. Then he ran into the bedroom and slammed the door shut.

A week later, Andrew announced that they'd all be going to Dartmoor.

'All?' asked Jessica.

'Yes. Clem, Felix and Jack have agreed to come with us. Pete's got enough room for all of us. And then we can see how we get on as one happy family.'

'You're crazy,' Jessica protested. 'What will Tom say?'

Tom said a lot. Mostly at the top of his voice. But it didn't make any difference. Half-term arrived, and together they set out for Dartmoor in Andrew Fraser's taxi. Jessica sat between Tom and Felix.

'If you two play up, I'll hit you with my plait,' she threatened.

Tom muttered under his breath non-stop for the first hour, then fell into a moody silence. Felix just stared out of the window.

Chapter Six

'Are we nearly there?' Jack asked for the millionth time as they drove along a bleak lonely moorland road. But this time no one answered, for the taxi suddenly slewed across the road, sliding, skidding, brakes screeching.

'Look out! Look OUT!' yelled Andrew, hanging on to the steering-wheel, trying to hold the mad car. At the back they were all screaming and shouting, falling forwards and sideways, shaken about, Tom thrown on to Jessica and Jessica on to Felix.

'What is it? What's wrong?' cried Clem at the front, clutching Jack, who was crying.

'I dunno,' Andrew shouted. 'I'm trying to hold it. But the car's gone mad. LOOK OUT, all of you!'

The car swerved back again across the road. Jessica saw a grass verge, a ditch, a stone wall, green, grey, white flashes, the dark fir forest behind as the car headed for the wall faster and faster, rushing to disaster, a crash, a smash. Stuck between Felix and Tom, she couldn't move, could only pray.

'Our father, which art in Heaven, save us now.'

She tried to scream but couldn't. Time was going slowly, stretching itself like an elastic band. They were moving and not moving and she knew she'd see that stone wall and those terrible trees for ever . . .

Dad! Dad! I don't want to die on Dartmoor! she screamed inside.

The taxi stopped on the grass verge, the wall a thought away. The horn blared. And then there was silence.

'It's the end of the world,' Jack whispered.

'No, it's not,' Clem comforted him. 'We're OK. We haven't crashed.'

'You all right back there?' asked Andrew. He was shaking.

'Yeah, yeah, I think . . .'

'What on earth did you do, Dad?' Tom cried.

'Nothing. Nothing, I tell you. It was the car.'

They scrambled out, needing air. Sweet, fresh, damp air. Everyone was stiff, shattered, legs aching after the long drive, to say nothing of the near crash. Jessica couldn't stop trembling. They *were* OK. And feeling terrible.

Andrew Fraser looked ten years older, his face white, lines drawn down it.

'We could all have been killed,' he muttered.

'But we weren't,' Clem said, matter-of-fact. 'We were lucky there were no other cars about. Come on, let's get the cab back on the road.'

'What really happened, Dad?' asked Tom.

'I dunno. I really don't. Suddenly it was as if the cab had a mind of its own. Or a mind of someone else's. I wasn't in control. Someone or something else was. It was terrifying.'

He shuddered.

'It's getting dark,' Clem warned.

'Yeah,' Andrew agreed heavily. 'I don't want to have to find Pete's cottage in the dark, for heaven's sake. Let's get going.'

He pushed his fingers through his hair so it stood up in tufts, his specs slipping down his nose. Jessica suddenly felt sorry for him, landed with all of them in this desolate place. She tried not to wish she was back at home.

Felix moved up behind the cab. They looked up and down the road to see what might have caused the near crash. There was nothing. Nothing at all except for fields, walls, trees and that bleak, flat, ordinary road, getting darker by the minute.

Jack wriggled as Andrew got into the taxi and Tom, Felix and Clem got ready to push.

'I want a pee, Jess,' he muttered. 'Please.'

'Well, go here.'

'Don't want people to see.' He glanced at Tom.

'I'll take you,' said Jessica. 'There's a gap in the wall. Come on.'

She swung him up, light as a leaf. The grass was wet as she stepped over the ditch, through the gap, into the wood and into terror. The wood was dark, lonely, full of silence and fear. Jessica, who never panicked, was suddenly so scared she could hardly move. Then a rush of wings came in the silence, and a wild cawing as dozens of rooks flew out of the wood, swooping down and over them.

'I don't like the birds,' cried Jack.

'Please, please be quick. Hurry up. Please.'

As he finished she snatched him up and ran through the gap, over the ditch and on to the road, where the taxi was almost ready to go. One of the rooks flew down and settled on the bonnet.

'Shove off,' yelled Tom. 'Horrible black thing.'

Felix tensed, but he said nothing as they scrambled back in. The road was still empty. Andrew studied the maps as the rook flew slowly away.

'The lane past Pete's cottage is somewhere on the left. He says it's fairly hidden, so keep your eyes skinned.'

'That's all we need on this crap holiday,' Tom grumbled. 'Getting lost now. What you staring at?' He turned on Felix. 'Look out your own window . . .'

Felix looked away without speaking and they drove off slowly, steadily, along the road in the old taxi-cab until they saw the lane and turned down it. Uncle Pete was there waiting as they drove up.

Chapter Seven

'Road rage,' said Uncle Pete, randomly picking out notes on his guitar.

'What d'ye mean? It couldn't be road rage,' Andrew spluttered. 'There wasn't another car or driver in sight.'

'Car rage, then.'

His guitar rippled.

'The car was sick of you lot after driving for miles, and I bet the kids were tiresome and the car wanted to throw you all out. Well, it's as good an explanation as any other.'

He began to play, ear-rings glittering in the firelight.

A burning log suddenly slipped down among the bright embers on the old blackened stone hearth, shooting sparks up the chimney and making glittering tiara trails in the crusty soot, and Jessica watched them fascinated, half-asleep, while Pete's guitar weaved magic in the firelight and candlelight. Nothing seemed to matter after Pete's wonderful meal except warmth, music and sleep. The cottage was sanctuary after the cold moor and the fright they'd had. They sat around the burning fire like stone age people in a cave. Jack slept on Andrew's lap on the wooden settle beside Pete. Clem dozed beside Jessica on an ancient sofa, half its stuffing hanging out. Tom sat upright at the table, not stroppy and cross for once. Somewhere in the shadows of the room was Felix, silent as usual, for he never said much except when Tom pushed him too far, went over the top.

Somewhere in the cottage a door or floorboard creaked. Jessica stirred.

'Don't worry,' Clem murmured from the other side of the sofa. 'It's this cottage. It creaks a lot, I noticed earlier. Like it's having conversations. It's nice here. I'll make some tea in a minute. Then we'll all wake up and I'll put Jack to bed.'

'I'll help,' Jessica answered, trying to push back the sleep.

'It's OK. I'll manage.'

But Uncle Pete heard and jumped up.

'It's my job. I'll make the tea for you.'

'No, you go on playing. Felix will help me.'

Felix loomed silently out of the shadows and followed his mother into the kitchen. Jessica half dozed off again, thinking that a few months ago she hadn't known Clem or Felix or Jack. Only a few months ago . . . when it all began.

Clem handed her a cup of tea. 'We must make some plans about what we'll do this week, Jessica.'

'That's up to Dad, really, I think.'

'I think he's so pleased just to be here with all of us, he'll more or less do what everyone wants.'

Tom stood up, pulling off his personal stereo. He'd been listening to it while Pete played.

'I'm knackered. Anybody care to tell me where I'm sleeping tonight? Not with *him*, I hope. Nor little wee Jackie, thank you.'

Pete jiggled a chord straight across his guitar.

'You're in the attic, Tom. I told you, remember? Next door to me. It's all ready. Felix and Jack are in the room on the right at the top of the stairs. Jessica's next door in what looks like a broom cupboard – sorry, Jessica . . .'

'I don't mind . . .'

'Clem and Andy here are in the caravan. OK? Does that suit you, Tom?'

'Fine,' Andrew said.

It almost seemed like Happy Families.

Jessica went up soon afterwards to her broom cupboard, which was OK, quite pretty really. Too tired to unpack, to read, almost too tired to undress, she climbed into bed, her head full of music and aching a bit, her skin too tight for what was inside it. As she drifted off she could hear the guitar and the sound of singing downstairs. They sounded happy. Good.

She awoke to another voice, like a rusty crow or something unlikely, singing loudly in her ear. She tried not to listen, burying her head under the covers.

'Wake up, Jess. Let's go look at FINGS.' Jack was shaking her awake. She got out of bed and pulled back the curtains. The sun was shining, they were on holiday, Dartmoor all around, waiting for them.

She carried Jack down the stairway, narrow and dark because of the door at the bottom, and lifted the latch into the living-room.

'Oh, no. Oh, no. Oh, NO!!!!!!'

Chaos. Stuff all over the place.

Nothing was straight. Mugs were broken. Glasses shattered. Pictures crooked and skew-whiffed. Rugs thrown everywhere. Chairs anyhow, one broken. Anything that could be moved, bashed, knocked over, had been.

She placed Jack carefully on the bottom stair.

'Don't move.'

Then she ran to the caravan to fetch her father. And Clem.

Chapter Eight

'No, I didn't do it! It wasn't me. It's not fair to say it was me. I didn't have anything to do with it.'

Tom stood there, hands stuffed in jeans pockets, answering his dad back.

'Dad, I believe him,' Jessica put in. 'Tom's not a liar, you know he isn't. If he says he didn't mess it all up, he didn't.'

'Why not ask him, then?' Tom jerked his thumb at Felix. 'Why just think it's ME?'

'Felix, did you vandalize Pete's room?' asked Andrew, and his voice was different from when he asked Tom – gentler, almost polite, but then Clem was there looking at them both. Felix was cool, very cool.

'No, I didn't, sir. I don't do that sort of thing. It's a waste of time and I'm not like that.'

'Perhaps somebody broke in. A burglar or somebody with a grudge against Pete,' put in Clem.

'Has anyone got a grudge against you, Pete?'

'Dozens of people. I make enemies all the time,' he grinned. 'You know that. It's a gift. Come on, let's skip the inquisition, clear up and forget it. This is supposed to be a holiday, let's enjoy ourselves. Relax.'

He waved his hands, smiling, trying to make everyone happy. He caught Jessica's eye and winked. But Andrew Fraser wasn't going to relax.

'Look, if either of you two *has* done it, own up now and we'll forget all about it.'

No one answered.

'Perhaps it was a mistake coming here in the first place,' he said, crumpling suddenly, sitting down and putting his hands over his face. Jack pulled them away.

'Bad piskies done it,' he said, pulling a horrible face until Andrew smiled at last.

'Yuck,' Tom muttered. 'How d'we know *he* didn't do it? Or Jessica, maybe?'

'Don't be silly,' said his father.

'I'm going to search the garden.' Pete's voice was loud and clear. 'Sherlock Peter Holmes, the great detective, will solve the mystery. There will be strange footprints in the garden, I don't doubt. Probably Yeti footprints.'

He pulled on a woollen bobble hat and went outside, the others following, except Tom who disappeared upstairs.

It doesn't feel like the 'Best Holiday of the Year', Jessica thought, more like 'Disaster Strikes Again'. Happy Families is just not gonna work.

After a bit: 'Can't see anything outside,' Andrew said from the doorway.

'We can't see any footprints,' Pete called out, ''cos it's all trampled flat anyway. That's my garden. But I forgot to lock up last night. I was enjoying myself too much. So someone could have got in.'

'I'd have thought you'd have a dog here,' said Clem. 'For a watchdog.'

'Well, I did. But he didn't like my music. He used to howl dismally every time I played. So in the end I gave him away to a farmer.'

'Shows what he thought of it,' grinned his brother, looking happy at last.

They started to tidy up the mess. The damage looked worse than it was and everyone cheered up as they cleared up.

'My stuff's so terrible you can't wreck it anyway,' Pete said. 'Only my music's valuable and that's up in the attic with me, safe.'

Breakfast and lunch had got mixed up as it was late, so everyone had just what they fancied and no one was arguing as they sat back deciding what to do with the remains of the day.

'What do you two want to do?' Pete asked

Tom and Felix. 'Just today, mind. You can't always choose.'

'Play football . . .' they both chorused, in agreement for once.

'I want to look at the moor,' Jessica said.

'Me too,' Clem added.

'OK – that's fine. I know a place quite near. It's too late to go very far today, as it gets dark so early.'

Felix, Jack and Clem went in Andrew's taxi, Tom and Jessica with Pete – no hassle there.

And so Jessica arrived at last – the moor stretched out all around her, miles of wilderness, misty, alien, lonely. She chewed her plait happily, all the spooky tales she enjoyed reading swimming around in her mind: *The Hound of the Baskervilles*, *Giants' Footprints*, *Jay's Grave*, *The Bottomless Bog* . . . I'm here! Jessica Fraser, me, and the mysterious moor.

'That bird up there, Pete? What is it?'

'It's a buzzard hawk.'

'Looks fierce.'

'It is. Very.'

'It's hovering, sort of.'

'Yeah, ready to drop on some poor animal below. Chop, farewell, little beastie. Welcome dinner to the buzzard.'

'Don't be horrible, Uncle Pete.'

'I'm not. It's just nature. Not pretty, not all flowers and singing and dancing and hey-nonny-no. Nature's cruel.'

'Oh. But, Pete, I hope there's *some* singing and dancing.'

'Can't we stop and have a kick around? I've brought the ball.' Tom's voice was impatient. He hated conversations about nature and so on. Boring, he thought.

'What about Felix? *Can* you two play together?'

'We don't. We'll play *against* each other.'

They stopped at the next flat stretch of ground. Everyone joined in, scrambling and kicking, especially Jack. But after a time Jessica backed away slowly and sat on a rock, watching the light fade from the hills and tors all around, while the others heaved up and down the wet moor, not missing her, until at last: 'Better get back. It'll be dark soon,' Pete yelled.

A black cloud, like a swarm of insects, filled the sky, swirling and turning like iron filings drawn by a magnet, and Jessica saw the rooks again, bringing terror like before. She counted one – two – three – four, but there were too many. They were only birds, but the panic feeling returned.

One of the rooks perched near, fixing her with its little eyes. She couldn't move. She felt the sweat rise on her face and prickle her back. What was this? What was the matter with her? It was only a bird. And she wanted atmosphere, didn't she?

Jack limped over.

'Jess. We're going now. Come with me to the car. Go away, rooks!'

The rooks flew off as she picked him up. He tugged at her plait. 'Gee-up, Jessy!'

As she got back into Pete's car she wondered what she'd been scared of. It wasn't like her. Rooks were noisy but harmless, of course. Of course.

'The story of Childe the Hunter is one of the best known legends of Dartmoor.'

Felix sat reading to Jack on the settle by the fire. Outside the wind was beginning to moan round Pete's cottage, bringing with it loads of Dartmoor atmosphere.

'Childe the Hunter was a rich man . . .'

'Seriously rich?'

'Seriously rich.'

'I wonder what it's like to be seriously rich?'

'Am I gonna read this story or are you gonna sit there talking?'

'You read.'

'. . . and this Childe Harold Hunter . . .'

'Was he a little boy?'

'No, he wasn't a little boy.' Felix was beginning to sound ratty. 'He was a man.'

'Why was he called child, then?'

'I think it's another name for Sir. He'd be a knight or something.'

'Sir Harold?'

'Yeah, I guess.'

'Go back to Childe the Hunter. Sir Harold's like a packet of tea.'

'A packet of tea? What's that supposed to mean, nut-face?'

'Groceries. Sir Harold's teabags.'

'You're a crazy kid. Let's just read, huh?'

'One more fing.'

'Wha-a-at? I wish I'd never started this.'

'Whereja get that book? It's old and nice and smelly.'

'It's one of Pete's. Found it down the back of a chair.'

'Uncle Pete.'

'Pete to me, Jack. He's not *my* uncle. Nor yours. Now for the last time, am I reading this or not?'

'You're reading it.'

'Childe the Hunter was a very rich man. He often rode over his lands on Dartmoor. One day when he was out hunting he got caught in a blizzard – wild like tonight, Jack – but much worse because it was midwinter then and snow began to fall on the moor and all around Childe

43

the Hunter. At first he tried to battle his way through the blinding snow, but it grew worse and worse. He could barely see his horse's head in front of him. Exhausted, at last, he decided to go no further but to wait till the storm had blown itself out, and he and the horse lay down in the shelter of a small gully. All night they lay there, and the following day and night, waiting for the storm to be over. But at last Childe the Hunter knew that he must soon die of exposure. He had to have warmth to stay alive, so in desperation he slew his horse, disembowelled it and climbed inside. Weeks later he and the horse's remains were found frozen to death. His tomb lies on the edge of Fox Tor Mire.'

Felix sat back on the wooden settle and grinned wickedly at Jessica, listening, fascinated.

Jack drew in a deep breath. 'What's disembubbled?' he asked.

'He pulled all its insides out,' Felix replied, straight-faced.

'What a horrible story!' said Jessica.

'Well, the moor can be a horrible place,' Pete put in. 'Like I said, Jessica, it's not all about piskies and wishing-wells. You have to be tough to be a survivor. Still do in fierce winters.'

'Bit like being black in Hackney,' grinned Felix, firelight shining on his face.

'But he didn't survive, did he?' Jack beamed. 'He was all deaded.'

'Supper's ready,' sang out Clem, before anyone could think of an answer to that.

Chapter Nine

Lying in bed later, listening to the wind whistling up over the moor, not dropping off to sleep straight away as she had the night before, Jessica kept going over and over that first talk to her father about Clem, Felix and Jack.

'Now, tell me . . . all . . . about it, Dad,' her head said as she lay in bed. 'Now tell me . . . all . . . about . . . it . . .'

But far away she seemed to hear Felix say, 'Childe Harold was a very rich man . . .'

'Now tell me all about it, Dad,' her head said again. Round and round. Everything going round and round.

'Childe Harold was a very rich man and he often rode over his lands on Dartmoor.' Felix again.

It now seemed that her father was reading her this in Felix's voice.

The words all turned round and round about in her mind.

'Tell me all about . . .' Drifting, drifting . . . sleep . . . sleep . . . sleep . . .

Oh! No! They were heading for the stone wall, the dark trees, oh, the rooks, the fear . . . I don't want to die on Dartmoor! she tried to say.

And woke. She'd heard something somewhere. Sweat poured over her and left her cold and clammy. There'd been something, some sounds downstairs.

Must be just someone stirring, getting a drink; Pete getting ready to go to bed. But no one had come up the stairs and past her room, she was sure.

Suppose . . . suppose someone had broken in. Suppose they were down below her, breaking, stealing . . .

Best be still. She slid down the bed, duvet piled high. Don't move. If you disturb burglars you could be murdered even if all the others were in the house. It had happened to other people. Cases too horrible to think about. Cruelty beyond belief. Lie still, Jessica. You're safe here. But *they* might come in the room and stand by the BED!! How could she go back to sleep thinking *they* might come and stand over her?

There was a bolt on the door. Yes, a bolt on

the door. Definitely. She remembered seeing it earlier. Get up quietly so that if anyone's there they don't hear *you*, push the bolt across, then get back to bed and GO TO SLEEP. That's the safest.

At the door she paused, opened it a little and listened. Everywhere was totally silent. Silent as the tomb; the grave; dark night on Dartmoor. Not a sound. Not a murmur.

Barefoot, not making even a rustle, she stepped down the stairs as cautiously as if she were walking on eggshells. The black was absolute because of the shut door at the bottom.

Slowly, silently, she lifted the latch, and slowly, silently, pushed the door.

Moonlight fell into the uncurtained room, patterning the carpet. A red log glowed in the grate. The wind had dropped and outside in the garden all was still. Nothing was stirring, not even a nocturnal beastie.

She was back up the stairs, door closed, and in her bed in a jiffy. Then sleep jumped her fast.

Great-Grandma Fraser's face was cracked wide open under its Edwardian hat covered in fruit and flowers, and her enormous lacy bosom splintered into a spider's web. Somebody had bashed Great-Grandma Fraser's portrait and done a great job.

'Don't you dare creep off upstairs!' Andrew Fraser bellowed as Jessica opened the door at the foot of the stairs and saw the wrecked picture.

'But I've only just got here!' Jessica shrieked back.

'I don't mean *you*, Jessica. No, I'm talking to your brother here. Asking him if he did *that* to a family heirloom.'

'Eh?' This was crazy.

Tom slouched against the settle, cross.

'Do you know if Tom could have done it, Jess? Or who is trying to wreck our holiday?'

'How do you know it's Tom? It might be Felix,' put in Clem, picking up Jack, who was crying.

Felix glared at her.

'Thanks, Mum. Whose side are you on?'

'I'm not on any side. Oh, don't cry, Jackie boy. It's all right. It's all right.'

Into all this the bobble-covered head of Pete appeared round the kitchen door.

'Toast, everybody! Loads of it, on the kitchen table. Get stuck into it. Please. For Pete's sake!' No one laughed. 'That was a little *joke*,' he groaned. 'What a miserable bunch you are.'

Glad to escape, Jessica helped herself from a huge buttery pile on the kitchen table. Honey, marmalade, peanut butter stood beside it. Tea and coffee and orange juice were laid out.

There's always food for comfort, Jessica thought, even if the house is crazy.

'Come on, the rest of you,' Pete yelled. As they began, he said, 'I always hated that picture. I loved our gran. Lovely lady. And she used to tell me about her mother, that old bat up there. Apparently she was a real tyrant. Used to beat her if she didn't do the housework properly. Mind you don't get that way, brother,' he addressed Andrew, who was looking at a piece of toast as if it might get its revenge and bite him back. 'So I'm glad that picture's smashed,' he concluded.

Andrew's face crumpled. Because he was really an old softy he hated telling people off, so he shouted and roared, then got upset and spluttered and stuttered. Jessica knew this. Tom didn't. Jessica felt she'd be more scared if Clem was angry than her dad.

'I don't give a brass monkey for the picture,' Pete went on. 'I'll get it mended and you shall have the great family heirloom, Andy. Anyway, I've got loads of pictures in the attic so I'll put something else up there.'

The phone rang.

'Sure,' Pete answered. 'Of course I haven't forgotten. Yes, the party's definitely *on*. Time? Oh, any time after eight.'

He turned and beamed at us.

'Hallowe'en tomorrow. October the thirty-first. And we're having a party, a ball, a thrash, a gig. We'll haunt the night away. Come on. Smile. Forget about smashed pictures. I know, we'll start again as if nothing had happened.'

Tom and Felix stared stonily at him as if he'd gone crazy.

'How long have we got to stay here?' Tom asked. 'How soon can we go home?'

'And which home would that be?' asked Felix bitterly. 'Where do I end up?'

I knew this holiday wouldn't be easy, thought Jessica, eating as much as she could to make up for it.

Chapter Ten

Logs blazed in the old hearth, candles flickered, food and drink were set up in the kitchen. There was cider and punch and home-made wine; spiders' webs, skeletons, cats, toads and snakes lurked in dark corners. It was Pete's Hallowe'en party and he and Clem had pulled out all the stops.

Jack was ready early. 'Calm down,' Clem said, but he couldn't, he was a Jumping Jack, a fizzy bottle, an exploding firework – he kept taking off his devil mask with the red horns and flicking the cat's tail Jessica had made him out of old tights. He couldn't sit still.

'Jessica, be an angel and read him a story. I want to get changed,' said Clem.

'OK – what about *The Three Little Pigs*, Jack?'

'No, no – I want Felix and another HORRIBLE story.'

'If you can find it, I'll read it,' Felix replied. 'It's hiding under the settle.'

Jessica curled up on the sofa to listen, dressed ready in a black top with black leggings, and a witch's hat hung with green hair, a big green plasticky nose which kept falling off and a broomstick she'd made out of twigs and an old stick. Felix opened the book. He wore a wolf mask and looked scary, Jessica thought.

'Which one?'

'That one,' said Jack, pointing. 'That's the one I want.'

'You're sure? It doesn't sound very nice.'

'I want a horrid one. Go on. Read. Read it, Felix.'

Felix took off his mask to read.

The Hairy Hands

'The most famous of all the Dartmoor legends is that of the Hairy Hands. This is a modern legend, having started some time last century, with tales of coaches and horses running off the road between Postbridge and Two Bridges near Bellever Forest. The coachmen said that a pair of hairy hands had seized the reins and wrenched them aside.

'Later, when cars came, the hands seized the steering-wheel in a grip of steel and caused the cars to crash. Even motorcycles weren't safe: one army dispatch rider ran into a ditch and later said that

*a pair of hairy hands had seized the handlebars
and steered the bike out of control.*

'*The last known sighting of the hairy hands was
at a caravan. The husband had dozed off, and his
wife was sitting writing when she suddenly felt
clammy with fear and to her horror saw two hands
with hairs on the joints appearing through the
window of the caravan. She sat stunned; then, just
in time, she made the sign of the cross and the
hands disappeared. Strangely enough, she said that
after the hands disappeared she felt a deep sense of
peace, so much so that when her husband wanted
to move the caravan somewhere else she refused,
saying that they were now safe.*

'*The hands have not been seen since. Perhaps
the woman somehow settled them for ever?*'

No one else was listening, just Jack and Jessica,
and as Felix finished the story they gazed at
each other, Jack's mouth open, eyes like saucers,
Jessica chewing her plait for comfort.

At last Felix whispered, 'D'you think that's
what nearly got us in the car on the way here?
Perhaps they're not settled for ever? Perhaps
they'll come again? For us?'

He and Jessica stared at each other as the
door was flung open. Pete's band had arrived,
and the cottage burst into talk, laughter,
snatches of song; instruments and clothes everywhere, Pete greeting everybody. Andy Fraser

stood there, glass in hand, laughing, Clem beautiful beside him. They looked like an item and Jessica suddenly felt left out as she tugged at his sleeve.

'Dad, Dad, I want to ask you something.'

He turned towards her but she only got half his attention. He kept looking at Clem, spectacular in a gauzy black dress with gold plaited in her hair.

Jessica shook his arm.

'Dad, the crash. I think I know what it was. Dad, listen. The crash. Felix read that story out of Pete's old book . . .'

'Jessica, you haven't got a drink.' Pete rushed up beside her. 'Can't have my favourite girl left out. What's your fancy – Coke, lemonade, orange, soft drinks, brandy?'

'Oh – Oh, Pete . . . oh, Coke will do. But Pete . . .'

'OK – I'll get it. Your wish is my command!'

Sometimes he's like someone out of a pantomime, thought Jessica. She shook her father's sleeve again.

'Dad – Dad, listen to me.'

'OK, I'm listening.'

But he wasn't. He was looking at Clem. Jessica's witch's nose was getting warm and soft and it fell off. She and her dad and Clem all bent down to pick it up and bump! Their heads collided. All I needed; keep calm, Jessica told herself as, scrambling round, she picked up the nose.

'Dad, I keep trying to tell you. I think I know what made us nearly crash . . .'

'Oh, Jess, don't go on about it. It's not often I drive badly but I was tired that day. Just enjoy yourself. Here's Pete with your Coke. Go and get yourself something to eat and have some fun. Where's Tom?'

'Upstairs,' Jessica said, walking away with her Coke into a dark corner. It was no use trying to talk to her father. All he could think about was Clem, Clem, Clem. They had no time for anyone else any more, either of them, tucked away in their honeymoon caravan. All they were thinking about was THEMSELVES, while Tom was upstairs alone, and Felix – who could tell what he thought about, but she knew he wasn't happy.

Jack, though, was still bouncy and he pulled at her.

'Come wiv me for food, Jess,' he ordered, and tried to get into the crowd in the kitchen.

'Look out! You'll get trodden on!'

Clem should be looking after him, she thought, guiding him through all the throng. *They don't care about us at all. We* don't want to be here. *We* don't want to be this whole new multi-racial family. She tried to get back to Felix, talk to him about what had nearly caused them to crash, as he seemed to be the only person interested. But Pete was talking to him and handing him a tambourine. Felix was grinning and waving it about. He was getting on well with people. Much better than Tom.

Turning away, she saw her father and Clem on the sofa looking into each other's eyes as if there were no one else on the planet! She remembered how happy Tom had been when they split, like the hero of a bouncy American comedy, and how Dad had moped, his tufts of hair sad and droopy, dark eyebags and never a smile.

What was worse? Tom on top of the world? Or Dad?

And how could it be sorted out? She felt that *she*, Jessica, would have to do it. But she wished that someone would give her a hand.

'Come on, Dartmoor, you with your magic tricks, help me, then!' wished Jessica Fraser, as she chewed her plait. Jessica Fraser, laid-back no longer.

Chapter Eleven

My name is Tom Bone
I live all alone . . .

Pete and the band played and sang songs and soon everyone was joining in, Felix happy with the rest.

Then, after the singing and the music, silence fell suddenly. You couldn't hear a sound, the wind must have dropped; it was so quiet, the curtains hung heavy and still. The logs in the fire were glowing embers, the candles had burned low, the food was almost gone. It was nearly midnight. They waited for Pete's old grandfather clock to chime twelve, then . . .

'Come on, come on, everybody,' called Pete. 'It's midnight so we've got to welcome in All Saints' Day after Hallowe'en. Come on, all of you.'

'Now when the Saints,
    Oh, when the Saints,
    Oh, when the Saints come marching in
I want to be there in that number –
When the Saints come marching in!'

Everyone clapped and sang. All Saints' Day had arrived.

'Now tell us a story, Pete. A spooky one!' someone called out. 'It's safe now.'

'Yeah. A scary for Hallowe'en.'

'OK, OK, everybody. Your Uncle Pete will tell a witching story at the witching hour. Draw nearer and listen. What was that you were reading earlier, Felix?'

'I didn't know you were listening,' he said.

'Oh, yes. I couldn't miss that one. It's different. It's modern. It's for real. Where is it?'

'Here. Behind me.'

'What a funny old book,' said Clem.

'Found it when I moved in. Must have belonged to the old boy who owned this place before me. It even smells funny. Here, sniff, Clem!'

'That's weird. I don't like it very much.'

'Stop sniffing and get on with the story,' someone cried.

'Right, here goes,' Pete began. 'This is the story of the Hairy Hands.'

Jessica didn't want to hear it again. A ghost

story like *A Christmas Carol* was OK, and she didn't really mind the old legends about giants and ogres and pixies and witches and the devil's footsteps. But the story of the Hairy Hands was different. It seemed real, modern, a today story. It could happen again. She was sure it nearly had. On that stretch of road they'd driven along in the twilight looking for Uncle Pete's cottage, the Hairy Hands had reached out for them, tried to get them. She shivered.

Maybe her father had just been driving badly because he was tired after a long journey. But he didn't get tired when driving. Driving was his job. He could drive for miles without tiring.

She wanted to go to bed. But she felt almost too shattered to go up. And too scared to leave everybody and the warmth of the fire. Dartmoor nights! They terrified laid-back Jessica. She wasn't very brave after all. No heroine, her. So she sat and listened, though she didn't want to.

'You will find it difficult to believe but someone drove me off the road. A pair of hairy hands closed over mine – I felt them as plainly as ever I felt anything in my life – large muscular hands. I fought against them as hard as I could, but it was no use, they were too strong for me . . .'

'That's a really eerie story,' someone murmured.

'It's near here, you know. My dad told me about it.'

'It's so modern. Do you think it's someone who hates cars and motorized transport?'

'A road protester ahead of his time? A green ghost?'

'No, I've heard there were always accidents at that spot. Horses used to bolt or stand absolutely still and refuse to move right way back when.'

'There've been a lot of accidents, then . . . ?'

'Oh, yes. But the whole area's frightening.'

'It looks ordinary. No stone circles or anything. No high tors.'

'Yeah, I know, but have you ever been into those woods at the side of the road?'

'Conifer woods are always gloomy . . .'

'It's worse than that . . .'

Jessica crouched back in her sofa corner, listening.

'Someone was killed crashing into that stone wall that runs along there.'

She remembered the wet grass, the grey stone wall rushing towards them, the dark secret trees . . . the awful terror . . . the feeling of panic as she'd held Jack.

Someone else was speaking.

'I went into that wood once and I've never been so scared in the whole of my life. I was absolutely paralysed and I thought I'd never be able to get out of there. I jammed up completely. I just couldn't move. Then, well – I said a prayer, I don't know which one but I was trying to say it over and over again and I managed to move a few steps and . . . and . . .'

'And what?' someone whispered.

'. . . I fell over. Into a sort of stream. My face went in the water. I was rigid with terror. But it saved me.'

'It saved you? How?'

'Yes. The shock of the cold water woke me up and I could move again, even if I was soaking wet. So I got out of there as fast as possible. And here I am.'

'Yeah. Here you are! Hooray!'

'I'll tell you what, though. I'm never going in there again as long as I live. And I don't drive along that road any more if I can possibly avoid it.'

Jessica had heard enough. She was sick of ghosts and Hallowe'en. She wanted home and the boring safe houses all around, the corner shop selling everything, sweets, food, lottery tickets. Like Tom upstairs, she wanted her old home, her old life, before *they* came and it all changed. But they say you have to go on. You can't go back. There's no going back. She'd seen how Dad was without Clem, you couldn't part them again; that was how it was going to be in the future and she and Tom would just have to get used to it. And Felix, she supposed grudgingly, trying to be fair. Jack seemed to like it and all of them too. But maybe that was because he was used to worse things, pain and hospitals and treatment. Poor Jack. Things had changed and they couldn't go back, ever. But she was homesick, not only for home but for the past that was gone.

They were all still talking about the Hairy Hands . . .

Jessica slipped into the kitchen and grabbed sandwiches and bits and pieces for Tom. Especially sausages. He loved sausages. She wished he'd come down from the attic instead of sitting there all alone. She wished he didn't have to fight everything all the time, even though it was his nature.

Quiet up the stairs! All the people who'd been sitting up there earlier were now gathered round the fire below. Jessica stepped quietly. She didn't want anybody to hear her.

Holding the plate, she knocked at the door. She didn't know why.

No one answered.

Up there on the top landing, it was very cold. She shivered, thinking how lonely and vulnerable were the people and the little houses on the huge moor. If it got angry like the mad giants in the legend it could fling them all off into space in a minute, into nothingness, all gone, troublesome dwarf creatures, people.

She wished her father slept in the cottage,

not in the caravan. She'd feel safer with him here in the house. But it was no good thinking like that. It was best to be *sensible*, laid-back Jessica.

She pushed open the door.

The room was cold and empty.

The window wide open.

Tom was not there.

Chapter Twelve

Jessica wanted to go with them. After all, he was her brother, closer to her than anyone except his father.

They'd gone through the house, the attics, the cellar, but he wasn't there. No Tom. Next they searched the garden and the outbuildings, calling for him, shouting, shining torches, then spreading outwards to the field and the moor and down the lane to the road.

People got into their cars, keen to search, afraid and worried. And Jessica wanted to go with them.

'He'll come to me more than to anyone else,' she told them when it was clear that he was nowhere near.

But her father asked her to stay with Clem and Jack, to be there if Tom came back and to answer the phone. They were arguing whether the police should be called or not as they went back into the cottage, where Clem was banking up the fire and clearing up.

'I want to be out with THEM,' she grumbled to Clem. 'After all, he is my brother, not theirs. I know what he's like and how his crazy mind works when he's in a mood.'

'She's right,' said Uncle Pete. 'Let her come.'

If I live to be a hundred, I'll never forget tonight, thought Jessica. She got into Uncle Pete's car with Felix, and her father went with two of Pete's friends who knew Dartmoor. The others followed in another couple of cars.

It's All Saints, not Hallowe'en now, Jessica thought. All the nasties will have gone. Tom's *got* to be all right. She pushed all thoughts of Dartmoor ghosts and Hairy Hands out of her mind. She wouldn't think about them. Not now. This was a different terror, a worse terror; Tom missing – perhaps in danger.

They drove through an enchanted landscape, for the full moon was high in the sky so that every tree, every rock, every bush, every far-off star was sharp against the sky as if you'd cut it out for a collage, with millions of pinpricks lit by white gold shining through. The night was so bright it almost seemed like those summer days when the sun's so strong the shadows are black.

'We should spot him easily in this,' Pete said.

'Look! There!' Felix shouted, but it was only a bush shaped like a boy. They drove through the narrow winding Devon lanes with their steep banks and high hedges, where you could hardly see anything except the bright night sky above, and sometimes over the rattly cattle grids on to the open moor and back again to the lanes, covering everywhere they thought Tom might have gone. From time to time they stopped the car and shouted, 'Tom! Tom! Tom!' into the night.

But he was never there, there was no answer and they drove on again. They met other cars and other people searching and stopped, to ask for news or if Tom had turned up at the cottage. But no.

Jessica strained her eyes to catch sight of him. Nothing could happen to him, surely? Could it? (Think of the things you see on television, whispered a voice, but she tried not to listen.) Not Tom. Even if he'd been stroppy, he'd always been so great, so full of energy, bounce and football until ... until Dad had met Clem. Please come back home, Tom. I'll be nice to you for ever and ever and stick up for you against Dad. Suddenly fury swept over her.

'It's all your fault,' she cried to Felix at the back. 'What right have you to come looking for MY brother? I wish I'd never laid eyes on any of you. He'd never have run away but for you. Why don't you go away and leave us alone? He was happy before you came!'

Felix didn't answer.

'Hey, hey, Jess,' cried Pete. 'Cool it a bit. It's hardly Felix's fault. He's not a bad kid as far as I can see and he didn't want to get caught in this any more than Tom does.'

Felix spoke at last. 'At least, Jessica,' he said, 'I am out looking for him. I don't – I don't want him to get hurt.' And he turned back to the window.

'Oh, sorry,' she sniffed. 'I didn't really mean it. Anyway, Tom could be awful even *before* you came. But, oh, I do wish we could find him.'

They drove on in silence alongside a wall, a forest of trees, the tors far away. Somehow it looked familiar.

'Pete, it's where we nearly crashed. Oh, take care!'

'Yes, I'm looking out. I know this place, but we're OK, don't worry. You can keep your fingers crossed, Jess, and say your prayers, for a lot of strange things do happen round here. We'll get out and have a look around, but you stay in the car if you're scared.'

'No! No! I'm even more scared of being on my own here. It's so spooky.'

They got out of the car. The bright night,

the black trees, the white road and the grey stone walls were all around them. Panic gripped Jessica. She could hardly move. This was a horror movie, but she wasn't watching it. She was right in it. Pete grabbed her hand.

'Hold on to me.'

Felix took her other hand with his, large, warm and comforting. She felt better – not good, but better, as they went through the gap and beside the stream.

'Tom, Tom,' shouted Pete. 'Are you there?'

'Tom,' cried Felix, his voice high and wavering.

'Tom,' she cried as well, but there didn't seem to be any sound coming out. Bright blackness, black brightness, everywhere. She thought she was going to pass out. Not her, it couldn't be.

'I'm going – I'm going . . .' she muttered and then together they all ran out of the wood, through the gap, and scrambled into the car and slammed the doors.

Pete said, 'It was no use staying there because Tom couldn't have. Could he? No one could.'

'This road's horrible as well,' Felix whispered, 'like the wood.'

'Yeah. I didn't believe what they said, but it's true. There's something wicked here. Let's get out of it.'

Uncle Pete – who never believed in things

being wicked or evil – started the engine and the car shot away like a cheetah in a wildlife programme.

'I'm going back home to have a drink. I need one. And we'll see if any news has come in,' he muttered. 'OK?'

'OK. Oh yes, OK,' they all agreed. 'Then we'll come out again. Won't we?'

The cottage was warm and welcoming. Clem had drinks and hot food waiting, Jack was asleep on the sofa. Jessica wanted to go to bed, she was shattered – sleep, please, sleep. But how *could* she sleep with Tom out there, lost and alone on the cold moor?

She dragged herself up to the bathroom and then, opening her bedroom door, she saw that the duvet had almost slipped off the bed and was hanging right down over the edge on to the floor. As she straightened it her foot went under the bed. That was funny, she had thought it went right down to the floor, one of those divans with drawers underneath. But she could push her foot further under. What was that? There was a space under the bed. There was something in that space.

Down on her knees she went, delving under all the covers, lots of covers, bedrooms being rather cold at the cottage. And what rotten lighting Uncle Pete had got. She couldn't see very well. But surely she could feel something there.

Curled up, fast asleep on an old blanket, lay Tom.

Chapter Thirteen

Andrew Fraser pulled Tom out from under the bed and hauled him down the stairs, Tom moaning sleepily and rubbing his eyes, looking like a ruffled dormouse, while his father went ballistic. That's when Jack woke up and crawled under the table to hide with a cushion, so he couldn't hear.

Tom wasn't answering – well, not at first.

'Dad, stop – let's all go to bed!' Jessica cried, but no, he was like a dog with a bone – Tom – and he was not going to let go. He wasn't going to stop for Pete, for Jess, not even for Clem. Pete got up and made fresh tea to be going on with. It was nearly dawn and Jessica didn't know whether she was coming or going. Nor, from the look of it, did Tom.

Andrew was rabbiting on about being made to look a fool, at which Tom woke up enough to say, 'Why? You don't usually mind, do you?'

'Tom! Tom!' cried Clem.

'I'm off to bed,' Felix said.

'Me too,' Pete added. 'If you two want to argue till it's light, feel free. Be my guests.' And off he went.

Clem got under the table, picked up Jack and carried him upstairs. Jessica followed. She didn't care if the sky fell in just then – she'd just use it as a cover while she slept.

When she woke much later the room was light. Slowly she crawled downstairs, made a cup of tea and curled up on the old sofa. The fire was black and it was cold, so she fetched her duvet and wrapped herself up in it.

She thought of Andy and Clem in the caravan. Suppose the Hairy Hands came for them, feeling their way up the windows in order to get at them? Somehow they seemed more at risk out there than in the house. The caravan wouldn't be much of a protection against DANGER. Were they safe? What could she do?

Not a lot, she thought, but she could take them a cup of tea. They'd like that. She got a tray and matching cups and saucers – not easy at Pete's place – and placed a tiny vase with a late-season rose out of the garden on it. She made a pot of tea and chose the best biscuits out of the tin, pleased that Jack hadn't come down yet. Then she walked across to the caravan. They'll be pleased, she thought. And when they'd had their tea she'd really make Dad talk about the Hairy Hands.

She was just going to knock on the caravan door when she heard Clem's voice.

'But, Andy, I've told you I want to marry you. I love you and there's nothing I'd like better, but I can't. Not yet.'

'Why can't you?'

'I've got to be sure it will work out this time.'

'Oh, I'm sure it will, Clem.'

'But it all seems so difficult. Felix . . . Tom . . . they hate each other.'

'No, they don't. They only think they do!'

'Well, what's the difference?'

The tea was going cold. Jessica knocked on the door softly, so softly no one could have heard.

'What we'll have to do,' her father said more loudly – he must have moved nearer the door, 'is fix a wedding date and then they'll all have to fit in. They'll soon come round, you'll see. And Jessica and Jack are fine. They get on like a house on fire!'

'I hope you're right.' Clem's voice was low, weary. 'But, you see, for years Jack's treatment has been the most important thing in the world that's had to be done – that – and getting a job.

Everything else has sort of slipped by a bit. Even Felix.'

'It'll be OK. You'll see. Don't worry, Clem. They're great kids. They know we care about them.'

'I wish I could be as hopeful as you!'

Jessica backed down the steps with the tray and just then a voice rang out from the kitchen door behind her.

'Jess – Jess. Why you out there? Wait for me. I'm coming too, Jess. Wait for me!' It was Jack, limping to join her as fast as he could. Jessica swivelled round.

Crash went the tray, biscuits flying through the air. The teapot threw a wobbly, pouring all over her pyjamas and slippers as Pete's only matching pair of cups and saucers smashed on the concrete path.

The caravan door flew open. Andrew Fraser stepped out in bare feet on to the rose's only thorn.

'Ouch!' he roared, hopping about, then, 'What *are* you doing?'

'I was only bringing you some tea. I wanted things to be nice instead of horrible!'

Then Jessica ran past Jack and up to her broom cupboard and bolted the door.

After a while there was a knock on the door and a burst of Beatles song.

'Your troubadour has arrived, lady,' called a voice that could only belong to Pete. Jessica opened the door and in he came, bearing a glass of milk. He was wearing his bobble hat and very long silver ear-rings.

'Your wish is my command, lady.'

'I suppose they sent you to calm me down.'

'Something like that. Tell her to calm down, they said. Don't be like Tom is what they told me to tell you.'

'Oh, I never stay mad for long.'

'What was the matter?'

'I didn't like what they were talking about. Us! As if we were parcels to be handed around. Nuisance parcels. Then Jack called to me and it all went crazy.'

'Are you all right now?'

'Yeah. What are they doing downstairs?'

'Well, Clem and Andy have taken Jack for a piggy-back walk and I sent Tom and Felix off in a different direction. You and I are staying in and cooking supper this evening so we need to organize things.'

'You haven't sent Tom and Felix out together, have you?'

'They've got a football to look after them and keep them in order. It'll work, Jess, you'll see.'

'I hope you're right. OK, I'm coming. What are we going to cook?'

'A delicious Chinese takeaway.'

'*What?*'

'Yes. Get dressed and we'll drive over to Moretonhampstead a bit later on and pick one up. We can always tell them we cooked it. They won't know the difference!'

Dressed and ready, she came downstairs.

'Pete, I hope Tom and Felix are OK out there.'

'Why? They're not babies.'

'They might kill . . . no . . . hurt one another. Or do some damage.'

'Oh, everybody takes too much notice of them. Half of it's just showing off. I should know – I'm always showing off.'

'But you're not horrible with it.'

'OK – if you're really bothered, Jess, run and get them. They're only in the field at the back.'

Jessica ran out through the trampled garden, through a gate and into the rough field at the back of Pete's cottage, where sometimes a pony grazed. But it wasn't there today. Neither was Tom. Nor Felix. No sign of them.

She ran on into the next field and on to a path leading to a wood, calling, 'Tom, Tom! Felix! Tom!'

Silence everywhere. She ran on further, heart starting to thump.

'Tom, where are you? Tom!'

She was at the other side of the wood now, coming into an open space dotted with granite rocks and gorse bushes.

'Felix! Tom!'

She ran on and on. She couldn't stop. Part of her thought she ought to get back to Pete and get him to search with her, but something was pulling her further and further on to the moor, where a finger of it reached towards Pete's cottage. She ran up a slope with a large boulder – a mini-tor – perched on top of it. If she climbed the little tor she'd get a good view all around and be able to see them, she hoped. She scrambled up the rock and looked ahead.

And then the rooks came, dozens of them, circling round and round in their strange wild swoops. Oh, no! Sweat drenched her as panic engulfed her – no, no, go away, horrible scary birds. One perched on a nearby rock and peered at her, head on one side.

'Go away, you wicked thing,' she shouted at it.

They swirled once more, in a sweep so huge it seemed to cover all the sky, and then were gone, leaving only a very pretty little brown bird hopping round the rock she stood on. Calmer now, Jessica stared all around and there below in a green dip she could see the boys. Scrapping like fury.

She leapt down from the rock, running

towards them and yelling, 'Stop it! Stop, stop, stop! Wait for me!'

But they weren't listening.

'I hate you – you stuck-up black pig!'

'You racist moron! I hate you too.'

They were screaming abuse and insults at each other, worse than she'd ever heard, and hitting each other so hard that Jessica flinched as if they were hitting *her*. She ran forward to stop them, but they pushed her back so that she sat down, furious and yelling just as loudly but knowing she hadn't got the power to stop them. So she looked round for a stick to bop them on the head, well, one of the heads. Right then she didn't care which one.

Tom grabbed Felix round the neck in a stranglehold. Felix struggled briefly, then threw Tom over his shoulder, sending him rolling on the soft green earth.

'Stop it now!' Jessica yelled. 'What's the matter with you two?'

Tom ignored her and tried to get to his feet, only to find that he couldn't. The soft mud underneath the green grass sucked at his legs.

'Hey, I can't move my feet,' he yelled.

'Rubbish! You're not bottling out of this now,' snarled Felix.

'Felix, he's right,' she pleaded. 'He's stuck.'

'No, he's not.'

'I'm sinking, you git.' Tom's knees had now

disappeared in the ooze. 'Pull me out, will you?'

Jessica shoved Felix out of the way. She couldn't believe it was happening.

'Well, if you're not going to help him, I am. Grab my hand, Tom.'

Her brother stretched out one of his arms. She pulled at it with all her strength, but it was no good. Tom wasn't budging at all.

'Felix, help me, please. He's too heavy for me.'

'Oh, all right,' shrugged Felix.

'You'd like me to sink, wouldn't you?' Tom shouted, nearly waist deep now.

'It has its appeal,' said Felix as he grasped Tom's other arm and started pulling as well. But they still couldn't shift him.

'This isn't any good,' Jessica said. 'This mud's like glue.'

'WILL SOMEONE GO AND GET HELP!' yelled Tom. 'You know, HELP!'

'All right. I'll hang on to him. You go,' said Felix.

'Don't leave me with him,' pleaded Tom. 'Can't you stay?'

'Oh, shut up,' said Felix. 'I'm stronger and I can hold on to you better.'

She left them clinging together, shouting insults, and ran back in the direction of Pete. She found him coming towards her, wondering where she was.

'What's up, Jess?'

'Tom's in a bog,' she blurted out, red and breathless.

'What? The stupid idiot. What's he playing at?'

'They were having a fight. Oh, please COME! We can't get him out.'

They rushed towards the bog, unable to see the boys at first. Oh, no! What if they had both drowned before they could be rescued?

'Where are you?' Pete yelled.

Two muddy brown figures gazed back at them, both half-submerged.

'He's pulling me in as well,' snarled Felix.

'I couldn't think of anyone I'd less rather drown with than you!' retorted Tom.

Pete came back, carrying a thick branch.

'Shut up and grab hold of this,' he said. 'You first, Tom. You're in deeper.'

'Why should he come out first?' grumbled Felix.

'It's OK. I'll soon have you out,' said Pete, to reassure Jessica as much as them.

With Pete holding the branch, Tom crawled slowly out, looking like the creature from the black lagoon, dark brown up to his chest. He lay flat out on the ground, exhausted.

As Felix was pulled out, he looked over at Tom and grinned suddenly.

'You're almost as black as me now.'

'Get lost.'

They were lying side by side, still squabbling but neither with enough energy to do anything more.

'What a sight you two are,' said Pete. 'By the way, what was the row about?'

'Football. He lost my ball. Kicked it right away into the woods,' muttered Tom. 'Then he said it didn't matter 'cos I'd never be any good anyway.'

'Oh, I might have guessed it would be about that. What else?'

'He kept going on about Manchester United being much better than Arsenal,' said Felix. 'I hate Manchester United.'

'And I hate Arsenal,' retorted Tom. 'Man United are brilliant.'

'I hate Man United, I hate Arsenal too,' sang Pete. 'Come on home, you two, and get cleaned up.'

'I hope Dad doesn't see you,' Jessica said. 'I think he's had enough upsets for one day.'

They tried to sneak in unnoticed, but unluckily for them Andrew was just returning from his walk with Clem and Jack.

When he saw the pair of them he was temporarily struck dumb.

His face, though, spoke a thousand volumes.

That night Jessica tossed and turned, but couldn't get to sleep. The story of the Hairy

Hands climbing up the caravan window unfurled in her mind like a horror video. She got up, went to the window and looked out at the garden.

Eyes straining, she peered outside where moonlight reflected over the garden, light and dark shadows, shapes, a shimmering glow. Scratching sounds outside. An animal? A bird? A rook? A horrible, scary rook? Or was it . . . the Hands? The scratching grew louder, seeming to come from the direction of the caravan. She knew she believed in the Hairy Hands even if others didn't. She was sure they existed.

She watched for a while, chewing her plait, but couldn't make up her mind what it was. Could have been a squirrel. At last all was silent.

Yawning, she made her way back to bed, finishing off the packets of crisps under the pillow before she fell asleep.

Chapter Fourteen

Pete's little book fascinated Jessica, held her under its spell. She couldn't put it down. It took her out on the wild fierce moor with its ghosts, witches, devils and monsters, its tors, its streams, its bogs, its ancient crosses and graves where someone always places fresh flowers. She read of the weird Wistman's Wood with its dwarfish trees and bulging, lichen-covered boulders where the red-eyed dogs of Death, the Whish Hounds, kennel during the day and at night go forth on their phantom ride with Dewer, who is the Devil.

'Whoever is unlucky enough to encounter the Whish Hounds dies within the year . . .'

'You OK there, Jessica?' Clem called out. They were all playing Monopoly, and for once no one was shouting or quarrelling or hitting anyone else.

'Jessica?' she asked again.
'Mm. Mm. I'm fine.'

'Dewer and his Whish Hounds hunt for the souls of unbaptized babies. There's the story of a farmer who had been spending a convivial evening at one of the little alehouses and was riding home late across the moor. Suddenly, through the gathering darkness, he saw the Whish Hounds. Full of Dutch courage, he called out and asked whether they had enjoyed good sport, inquiring what they had caught. The Devil laughingly replied that he would make the farmer a present of their kill, and threw him a bundle. The man tucked it under his arm and rode home. When he dismounted on his own doorstep he undid it. Inside was his own child – dead.'

'Sure you're all right, Jessica?' Andrew asked, pausing in the game.

'Mm. This book's scary.'

'Oh, you don't want to take any notice of all that,' Uncle Pete laughed. 'Load of old cobblers. Come and join in here, instead.'

But no, she was hooked. Once she'd thought Dartmoor magic meant pixies and wishing-wells and Tom Pearse riding on a grey mare. But not any more. She read of black witchcraft and the Evil Eye, and magic circles and charms and spells and wart-curing. She read about Vixana, the Witch of Vixen Tor, of Cranmere Benjie, the Legend of Brentor Church, and of Grey Wethers. She read about the Hound of the Baskervilles, and wicked Lady Howard who haunts Okehampton Castle, and Berry Pomeroy with its many ghosts, the most haunted castle in England, most terrifying in bright sunlight.

And the Hairy Hands.

Always she came back to the Hairy Hands – a ghost story different somehow from the others, one that had something to do with all of them, that she felt was intended for them. She turned the page and there was another telling of the strange story.

'By the Cherry Brook, close to the very centre of Dartmoor, and a few hundred yards from the main road, was a gunpowder factory. Now gunpowder was being used more and more for blasting away granite for building from the many Dartmoor quarries. Because it was so dangerous that even a spark could blow the whole place up, the best place to put the factory was far away from any other houses and cottages. So, a mile from Postbridge, and close to two small streams, the Powder Mills were built and many people worked there.

Carlo, an Italian, found work there. He was hard-working, conscientious and popular with his workmates at the Powder Mills. The rules under which the men worked were very strict. The men were told to wear soft leather footwear or sheepskin slippers whenever they were inside any of the buildings because any spark from a hobnail boot would cause an enormous explosion.

Carlo enjoyed the work, dangerous though it could be. But on the way home one day he realized he had forgotten his lunch tin. He began to trot back towards the mills. They were now deserted except for one or two who were left in charge during the night to make sure there were no intruders, gunpowder being very expensive. Carlo knew exactly where his box was, so he had no need to stop. But he forgot to change his shoes. A spark from his nailed boot fell on a stack of barrels which quickly ignited and exploded. Poor Carlo. He was blown to bits, and it is said that his hands landed on the main road from Postbridge to Princetown. It is said that they still haunt the road there. But then, there are many stories about the Hairy Hands.'

In Pete's warm room, Jessica shivered, glad the others were all there with her as she read the strange, old-fashioned tale that yet, she was sure, carried its message for them. We were meant to come here to Pete's shabby, funny cottage, as if we were caught in a web waiting for something to happen; to sort out our muddle, she hoped, all with parts to play, Uncle Peter as Merlin the Magician, and the evil Hairy Hands lurking in the background . . . brrrrh . . .

'I've won,' cried Jack.

'Only because we let you,' answered Tom – no, it was Felix saying that, surprise, surprise.

'At least we didn't have a fight over it,' Andrew put in.

'Keep your fingers crossed,' Tom answered. 'There's time yet.'

'No, no – enough's gone on already,' Pete grinned. 'You certainly keep us on our toes, Tom . . .'

'It's not just me! Not just my fault . . .'

'That's enough! Let's work out what we'll have for supper. Jess can tell us. She's been resting over there with that book while we've been toiling over this difficult board game.'

Jerked back into everyday life, Jessica marked her page with a scrap of paper and said, 'It's a wonderful book, even if it's a real frightener.'

'Oh, don't start her off!'

'Jessica, we don't want any more tales about the Hairy Hands or spooks, not now. Just choose what you want for supper!'

'Me? Oh, everything. And then some more, please.' She chewed her plait at the thought.

'Jessica,' Clem laughed. 'Which do you like best: food, spooks, or books?'

'All of them, all the time,' cried Jessica.

'Well, why don't we have that Chinese take-away we never got around to yesterday?' Pete said. 'Would that suit everybody?'

They all agreed, even Tom and Felix, who both seemed quite relaxed tonight. Perhaps the fight and bog episode had taken the malice out of them for the moment. How long would it last?

Pete and Jessica set off for Moreton-hampstead to get the long-delayed Chinese meal. After all the spooky stories the moor showed its friendly side, gentle and beautiful as they drove along in the twilight.

'This is why I live here,' Pete said at last. 'Town life's not for me.'

They arrived back at the cottage with plenty of Chinese grub – spare ribs, sweet and sour, chop suey, chow mein, prawn crackers, stacks of rice and everything, as Jessica said.

Jack was waiting in the hall for them as they got back, and hungry fingers dished it out and tucked in eagerly, the room filled with the sound of munching. It was the happiest evening they'd had there so far, thought Jessica.

That night she had the first good night's sleep since they'd first arrived at Pete's cottage.

It'll be OK, she thought as she dropped off. No more trouble.

Chapter Fifteen

'Where do you all want to go today?' asked Andrew Fraser.

'Wistman's Wood,' Jessica said hopefully, eating toast, chewing her plait and reading *the* book all at the same time.

'Where the heck's that?' asked Tom. 'Can we get a game there? Otherwise it's a waste of time.'

'You'll get your game,' replied his dad. 'But we'll visit Wistman's Wood *first*.'

'Is this place far? Have we got to drive for miles? And I hope it's not one of these touristy places full of horrible little kids.'

He glared at Jack, who glared back and stuck out his tongue. Tom crossed his eyes, waggled his ears and growled so fiercely that Jack hid behind Felix.

'Watch it, you,' Felix warned.

'You can all watch it,' Andrew frowned. 'Any trouble and there'll be no football today. And I mean it. I'm going to take a firm line with you all.'

Tom sighed heavily and raised his eyes heavenwards just as . . .

'Has anyone seen my handbag?' inquired Clem, coming in. 'I've looked everywhere and I can't see it.'

'When did you have it last?'

'I can't remember . . .'

'Come on, everybody, let's look for it,' said Andrew.

They all started to search, even Jessica, leaving her book, except Tom, who sat chanting, 'Boring, boring, boring' and 'Why are we waiting' until his father hauled him to his feet.

'You useless . . .'

'Dad, don't hurt him,' Jessica said gently to him, then swung her plait round to hit Tom.

'Ow!' he yelled. 'That hurt more than any-thing HE can do.'

'Serves you right. Get looking.'

'I don't want to look for her stuff. I didn't lose it.'

Jack hobbled over and tried to kick him with his heavy boot. Tom moved to push him but Clem swept the little boy up quickly.

'Don't you dare!'

And at that moment Felix came in with a dripping polythene bag.

'It's here,' he said. 'It was in the outside loo.'

He fished out the handbag, which was unharmed, fine – not even wet.

'Somebody did this. You, Tom! You're trying to wreck everything!' cried his father.

Tom's face was angry, red and crumpled.

'Yes, I'd like to wreck everything – but I didn't put that thing in the bog. You know why? I wouldn't touch anything of hers. That's why!' he shouted. 'Oh, can't we go home?'

'How do you expect anyone to sleep in all that racket?' Pete stood yawning in the doorway.

'What's wrong now?' he added. 'Oh, don't tell me, I don't want to know. Please – let's all have a cuppa while we sort this one out . . .'

'Is your bag all right?' asked Andrew anxiously.

'Yes – not damaged. Everything's safe in it. Jess, get rid of this horrible polythene bag for me, will you?' Clem was almost in tears.

'Look, this isn't going to work. As Tom says, let's all just go home. To our own homes,' she said.

They all started to talk at once, except for Jack, who decided to sit under the table clutching his cushion.

'I want to go to Wistman's Wood,' Jessica said. 'Then we can go home.'

'Maybe it was an accident,' Felix put in. 'Mum, you know you forget things . . . We don't have to go home yet.'

'Don't tell me you're enjoying yourself, bo,' said Pete. 'You astonish me.'

'Well, it's not that bad . . .'

'That's because you don't keep getting accused of things you haven't done,' shouted Tom.

'Let's have that drink . . . then we'll sort it out,' said Pete.

From under the table a voice said, 'Want to go to the Wishy Wood.'

'It's not Wishy – it's Wistman's,' Tom said. 'Get it right, stupid.'

'Stupid yourself.'

'It could be Wishy,' Jessica answered. 'Hounds from Hell kennel under it and they're called the Whish Hounds. They're terrible creatures.'

Andrew Fraser took a deep breath.

'OK, let's all have another try. But, Tom . . .'

'Don't say it,' Pete interrupted. 'But this is my house and if it's mucked up by you lot once more I'll be really angry and there'll be trouble.'

'Yes, please, one more try,' Clem pleaded. 'I don't mind about the handbag. It doesn't matter.'

'I shan't be going with you today. Going to set up another gig,' Pete yawned. 'See you later. Oh, and try not to *exterminate* each other!'

And so the Frasers and the Pattersons set off again for football – then for Wistman's Wood.

Trying once more to make Happy Families work.

'Do you *have* to?' asked Andrew.

Because of the row over the handbag, Tom and Felix had forgotten to bring a football with them. So now they were kicking stones, and there were plenty to kick on the rough lane leading to Wistman's Wood.

'No, you can't drive right up to it,' said Andrew when Tom complained that walking was boring. 'You'll have to go on your own two feet.'

What Tom and Felix did then with their own two feet was to kick, dribble, left, right, round and round, flicking pebbles and stones off trainers and catching them again, each one watching the other out of the corner of an eye in case he'd worked out a new skill. Cries of 'Yes,' 'Now,' 'Wow,' 'Brill,' 'Wicked,' 'And how,' and sometimes 'RUBBISH' rang through the air. Jessica tried to join in at first, hoping it would turn into a game for everyone, but the two boys were in a mood where no game could last long and as they tried to score over each other, spite and malice and anger caught them and dust, grit and stones flew. Danger was in the air with the flying feet and debris.

Jessica dropped out of the game.

'Look out!' shouted Andrew, with Jack on his

shoulders, as he just managed to dodge a sharp bit of Dartmoor granite.

'You two are a menace,' Clem protested. 'Just be careful!'

'You lot whinge when I do something and whinge when I don't,' shouted Tom, kicking a stone really high and just missing her. Felix hit him on the knee with what looked like the head of a mini stone-age axe.

'Leave it out,' yelled Andrew.

'If you don't stop, we're going straight back to Pete's house.' Clem didn't raise her voice but they quietened down then, just dribbling gently along at last.

And now the morning was grey and damp and very quiet. It was further to the wood than they'd thought and after a while they slowed down, walking steadily along the rocky path. An elderly couple with white hair and stout walking shoes and sticks passed them, and two teenagers in T-shirts, plimsolls and old ragged jeans, their arms wrapped round each other. Almost, they could have been the last survivors in a story. November world, not even a bird above in the low looming sky. Perhaps, thought Jessica, everyone in the world's dead except the people here and us.

'Come on, Jessica,' called her dad. 'Stop daydreaming. We're at the Woods and there aren't any Hairy Hands here.'

*

Andrew was reading from a guide book. They'd found a sheltered spot among the boulders and the dwarfish, twisted trees and eaten their sandwiches and fruit and crisps there, a happy picnic outing.

'It's unlike any other wood in the world,' he read, 'mysterious, strange and haunted.'

Tom had stuffed his fingers in his ears but his father didn't notice.

'Like it? Worth coming to see?' he asked.

'Great. Wicked,' Tom called out, pulling out his fingers.

'That's amazing! You actually like something.'

'Yeah. It's a dwarf wood. A wood for dwarfs,' drawled Tom, looking at Jack.

'It's a bit cold for picnicking. Let's explore,' Clem said, leaping to her feet and packing away the picnic. Jessica helped and then went down to look at the river with Jack. But he was coughing a bit and shivering in the wispy mist that trailed over the water. Clem came and picked him up. They all wandered around exploring but now the mist lay all over the river and white spirals twirled round the trees and rocks, and put tiny beads on scarves and anoraks. Even their voices sounded different, padded and muffled.

They headed away from the water and up

the valley. Jessica felt peculiarly tired, her feet dragging as they forged uphill. Jack whimpered, carried on Andrew's shoulders now. Wistman's Wood and a November picnic had been a bit much. But at least Felix and Tom were quiet – the outing had even tired them out as well.

Jessica tried to go faster but the trees and rocks seemed to hold her back with their wispy trails. The others pulled ahead, Clem and Andrew singing nursery rhymes to keep Jack happy. Jessica could not keep up with them; their figures disappeared into the mist and the singing faded.

'Wait for me,' she cried, for now she could neither see nor hear the others. She tried to hurry. But Wistman's Wood was holding her back, she couldn't get going. Something jerked at her neck. She almost screamed. It was her scarf, caught on a thorny bush.

'Come *on*, Jessica!' her father called from far away.

'I can't. I'm trapped!'

She pulled at the scarf as panic set in, but the thorns tightened their grab. She pulled and tugged, tearing her hands on the thorns, ever more hopelessly hooked as red blood spurted and the scratches stung and bit. She breathed deeply, trying to bury the panic fear, then licked her fingers and began slowly and carefully to unfasten the scarf. She would have left it behind but it was her favourite, given to her last Christmas by her father.

At last she was free and she'd got the scarf safely off the thorns. She looked round. The mist was all about her now, and thick. She was alone, cold, lost.

'Wait for me! Wait for me! Please!' she wailed.

She tried to run, stumbled, bashed herself on a rock and fell, weeping and sobbing.

At last she pulled herself up by a branch and found she was looking into the red-rimmed eyes of a huge, black dog.

'Dad! Dad! The Whish Hounds!' screamed Jessica.

Chapter Sixteen

Pete's cottage seemed empty and forlorn without him in it as they collapsed inside, tired, dispirited and already hungry again. But Clem rustled up food while Andrew got the fire going and, eating, they relaxed, except for Jessica, curled up in the corner of the sofa. The Whish Hound had turned out to be a large black labrador called Flossie, harmless and sloppy, her owners, a pair of middle-aged walkers, said, as they calmed Jessica down and reunited her with her family. Tom's grinning and her father's annoyance as her rescuers told him and Clem off for not looking after her properly had made her want to hide away right beneath Wistman's Wood with all its boulders and dwarf trees, even if she encountered the terrible Dewer with all his Hounds underneath it. Anything, she felt, anything would be better than hearing, 'She's obviously a nervous, highly strung child . . .'

'No, she isn't,' protested Tom.

'. . . who needs careful handling. Our dear Flossie is the gentlest creature in the whole wide world and was only coming to help the poor child because she was crying and making a fuss.'

Clem tried to say that Jessica was usually very sensible. The two hikers took no notice whatsoever but continued speaking about the need for caring for others.

'Somehow I think they were teachers,' Andrew muttered, when they'd finally gone. He was ruffled.

'I'll talk to *you* later,' he said to Jessica. 'When we get in.'

Which is why she sat in a miserable heap on the sofa – waiting for a lecture. But when they'd finished eating Tom and Felix came in and sat on either side of her and Jack climbed on her lap and put his arms round her.

'See, Jess, you've got bruvvers,' he whispered. 'Don't cry.'

'She never cries,' said Tom. 'She'll probably hit Dad with her plait. And I'm her *only* real brother, see.'

'I want to talk to Jessica. Go and play somewhere else, you three.' Her father cleared his throat.

She waited and looked at him and suddenly realized he hadn't a clue what to say and that he was still her dear old dad, even if he did seem to have changed lately. There wasn't really any need to worry.

'You've changed lately,' he announced, too loudly, and then dropped his voice hurriedly. 'You used to be such a sensible grown-up girl and now, you're doing all this . . .' He vaguely waved his arm in the air.

'All what, Dad?'

'Well, I dunno. All this Hairy Hands and imagination twaddle. It's not like *you*. I know some kids love it and there's a lot of it about these days . . .'

'A lot of what about, Dad?'

'Oh, you know, spooks and things. I didn't know we were going to come in for all this Hallowe'en piffle – just like Pete, I must say – when we came on holiday. I came for us all to have a lovely time and get to know each other really well . . .'

Jessica, trying not to look at Tom pulling funny faces from the other side of the room, said, 'But we don't want to get to know each other really well. I like Clem and Jack and Felix is all right, I suppose, but I don't really want to know them any better.'

Here Felix suddenly pulled a face at her. She put out her tongue in return.

'Really, Jessica! Have you gone crazy, child? Don't pull faces at me.'

'You know, Dad, I think you'd be all right as a school teacher again!'

'This is ridiculous. Now listen, this is my last word on the subject . . . There are no such things as spooks, ghosts, spirit hands or anything else. Real evil is in people's nature, what people do, cruelty, crime, robbery, torture, abuse, lying . . .'

'Don't go on, Dad. Please.'

'. . . not in evil spirits. Get me?'

'Yes, Dad.'

'Have you anything to say, Jessica?'

'Can we go home tomorrow, Dad? It's not a very good holiday, is it? And please don't grumble at me any more!'

'Oh, I'm sorry. Oh, Jessica!'

'Suppose we all have a cup of tea and some of Pete's delicious cake?' said Clem.

'Yes,' they all yelled.

'You can breathe now. The trial is over!' Clem laughed and Andrew managed to smile.

'Do you really want to go back home?' he asked, some cake-filled minutes later.

'Yes, please . . .' said Jessica.

'But we haven't seen Dartmoor prison! One more day, please, sir?' Felix asked.

'Well, I could show Jessica where real crime can be found,' her dad replied slowly. 'Let's go and look at reality. Not much ghostliness about prison.'

*

Dartmoor prison looked like you'd expect – horrible. They stood staring at it, grey, gloomy, one of the world's sad places.

'Imagine living here,' Jessica said.

'Well, plenty do,' Tom grinned, jerking his thumb at the great granite building.

'I meant living here because you worked here, trying to make believe it was just ordinary, like other places.'

'It's got houses and shops, and a church and a garage,' Felix said. 'So there must be ordinary people here.'

Andrew said, 'You get used to it, I suppose. You can get used to anything in time.'

Tom glared. 'Oh, no, you can't.' Felix glared back, then turned away.

'Who lives in that BIG place?' Jack asked.

'People who've done bad things,' said Andrew.

'Well done, Dad,' muttered Tom. 'I wondered how you'd answer that one.'

'I don't want to live there,' Jack went on.

'Then you'll have to be good.'

'Tom and Felix aren't good. They're somfink else. Will they have to live there?'

'No, of course not.' Clem sounded cross, for once. 'Look, can we move? I don't like it here.' Like Jessica, she hadn't much wanted to come in the first place, but Felix and Tom were so keen.

'OK. OK. I only came because the lads wanted to see Dartmoor, the famous prison. And to show Jessica the real thing – not fantasy.'

'Where can we buy a new football? What we really need is a new football!' cried Tom, bored with such talk.

Felix grinned. 'And I'm with you for once, but *you* lost the old one, not me.'

'No, I didn't. *You* kicked it in a wood,' replied Tom.

'Don't you two start again,' said Clem. 'Let's go.'

They ran back to the car. It was cold, and a pale spangly mist still hung everywhere in tiny droplets. The moor here was harsh and unwelcoming, an alien planet, life on Mars. They'd driven in Andrew's taxi, for Pete was still at the gig in Cornwall with his band. Then they carried on to Tavistock, where Andrew thought they could buy a football, driving through different hills, different tors, the highest, wildest part of the moor, a thousand miles from home, thought Jessica, but wonderful.

Away from the prison the sun straggled through, and they sat outside for a pub snack, then wandered round buying little gifts and postcards. Tom bought a card to send to their gran, up north. 'Wish you were here,' he scribbled, drawing an arrow pointing at a view of the prison. Then he and Felix each bought a football with their money.

'Now they'll argue about which one to use and which one is the best,' Clem whispered to Jessica. They found a park where they could play, but Clem and Jessica found a seat in a sheltered spot and talked, trying to get to know one another, reaching out, perhaps a bit too far, for Jessica suddenly came out with, 'Why are you with Dad? You're glam but he's so ordinary, nice but scruffy.'

'He's the kindest and gentlest person I know. Look at him helping Jack join in the game and not feel left out.'

'Yes, he's nice. But not to Tom. Not lately.'

'I think – I hope we'll all settle down.'

'Will you get married, then, Clem?'

'Perhaps. If I'm sure it will work.'

Jessica kept on. Perhaps she shouldn't have, but she knew hardly anything about this family they were probably going to be part of and she was curious.

'Are you still married to Felix and Jack's dad?'

'No.'

'Then you *can* marry Dad?'

'Like I said, Jessica, only if it will work.'

'Is Felix like his dad?'

'Felix is more like me, really. Jack's like his dad. He's got his grin. But he's nicer.'

'Do they miss him?'

'No, I don't think so. I hope not. He wasn't a very *kind* person, Jessica.'

But then the lads arrived, red-faced and breathless, and stopped their conversation.

'Dad. Dad.'

'Yes, Jessica?'

'Can we stop at Powder Mills?'

'Oh, no, boring, boring,' groaned Tom.

'Look, you've had what you wanted. I think she should have her turn before we go back home.'

'Well, I'm not going round the place. *Dead boring.*'

'You can stay in the car, then.'

'Suits me.'

'Why do you want to go there, anyway?' Felix asked.

'Just want to look round. I've read this account that says the Hairy Hands began there at Powder Mills – a man with hairy hands was blown up there and his hands landed on *that* road and it's been haunted ever since.'

'Jessica! You're obsessed with this Hairy Hands thing,' said her father.

'It's rubbish,' said Felix – he wasn't as shy as he'd been at first.

'Do we have to stop there?' Tom put in.

'Yes! You two can stay in the car. And shut up.'

'I come wiv you, Jess,' smiled Jack.

'Me, too,' Clem added. 'There's a gallery where they sell pots. I'd like to see it. Maybe buy one.'

'Yuck,' muttered Tom.

They went down the drive to Powder Mills but everywhere was shut – out of season by now. Andrew parked in front of it while Clem, Jack and Jess got out of the car and looked round, though there was little to see with it closed. They walked across a tiny bridge, a stream running under it. Jack dropped some stones into the water. Not far away, Jessica could see a gully half-hidden by gorse bushes and dwarf trees.

'Look – there's a cannon,' cried Jack, and they went over to look at it – a little cannon on a wooden stand.

'They put the powder in here . . .' he put his arm down in front of it, 'lit it and BANG BANG BANG! You're deaded.' He was laughing his head off.

Overhead a helicopter whirred and then another.

'I wonder what they're doing,' Jessica said to Clem, who moved towards Jack to take him back to the car.

'Patrolling, I expect.'

Jessica looked round once more – but where were the rooks? Where was her usual sweaty panic? Nothing. Nothing scary at all. Clem and Jack were already back in the car.

It seemed to her a dark shadow stirred in the gully. Curious, she stepped towards it.

'Jessica. Come on, it'll be getting dark soon,' her dad cried. 'We're all waiting for you.'

She looked again for the dark shadow. Nothing. Yet she was certain something had moved there, something large, but not an animal.

'I'm coming,' she cried, and ran as the helicopters circled round again and then again.

It grew dark on the way home, but Jessica felt happy. Pete would be back from his gig and the cottage was always warm and welcoming with him there, but, best of all, they'd be going home the next day. She could see her friends, sleep in her own bed, listen to her own CDs, read the books she'd left behind. She'd finished Pete's little book. Good. She'd be sensible laid-back Jessica again.

Pete's car stood outside the cottage, its right-hand front bumper bashed in.

They rushed inside. What had happened?

Pete lay collapsed on the sofa.

'Pete, Pete,' cried his brother. 'What's happened to your car?'

Pete didn't answer. He just looked at them,

his eyes shocked and staring. Then he reached out and took Jessica's hands.

'You were right,' he whispered. 'You were right all along.'

'What is it?' she cried, thoroughly scared.

'The hands. The Hairy Hands . . .'

He let go of hers and stood up.

'I'm sorry – sorry, all of you. I'm shattered. I'm going to sleep for a bit. The late night gigs and then – then this wall. Sorry. I'll talk to you later, Andy. Take care, you kids. 'Bye. Help yourself to . . . things.'

Slowly, like a very old man, he went up the stairs.

Chapter Seventeen

They stood looking at one another in silence, then Tom said, 'What's he on about?'

'Not now, Tom. Let's make some supper and get Jack ready for bed. Don't, don't talk about it now. I'll go up and see he's settled in a minute. See if he's OK,' said his father.

Quietly they did as he said, and were just going to sit down to eggs and beans on toast cooked by Jessica, lovely comfort food, she thought. Clem was undressing Jack. Jessica had blanked her mind, feeling she couldn't take or cope with any more. She just hung on to the thought of going home tomorrow; then everything would sort itself out.

Someone knocked at the door. Jessica, not yet sitting down, opened it.

'May we come in?'

Two policemen stood in the doorway.

'What is it?' asked Andrew, leaving his eggs and beans.

The policemen took out their ID cards. The Frasers and the Pattersons sat frozen for a moment, then Tom and Felix began eating as fast as they possibly could, as if they wouldn't be allowed to finish. Jessica just stood there, scared. What was wrong now? What had they done?

The big balding badger-like one spoke.

'I'm Police Constable Mudge and this is Police Sergeant Skinner, sir!'

Sergeant Skinner was thin, sharp-eyed and foxy. His eyes needled round the room, taking in Clem, Felix and Jack, Tom and Jessica.

'Finish eating,' he said.

The boys had finished anyway, but Jessica didn't even feel like starting. She backed towards her favourite place on the old sofa and Jack got down and went to her, curling up with his arms round her.

'We're here to warn you, sir,' Sergeant Skinner went on, 'that two convicts have escaped from the prison today and we think they're hiding in the vicinity, so we're checking . . .'

'. . . the helicopters. That's why the helicopters are out,' Tom interrupted. The sergeant took no notice of him.

'. . . everybody and every house. Can you say

if you've seen anything strange or peculiar going on round here?'

All the time, all the time, Jessica thought crazily.

'Well, we're only on holiday here. For a week,' said Andrew, almost smiling. 'So that's what your call is about?'

'Did you think it was about something else?' glinted Sergeant Skinner. 'Have you perhaps got something else on your mind? Something you want to tell us?'

Andrew's tufts were standing up on his head.

'No, no, no.' He waved his hands about.

They must have noticed Pete's bashed-in car, thought Jessica. She held Jack tighter. He was falling asleep, tired out, but struggling to keep his eyes open to watch these strange and wonderful policemen.

The older one, bigger and more amiable-looking, spoke.

'You're on holiday then, sir? Been sight-seeing?'

'Yes, we went to look at Dartmoor prison. The boys were very keen to see it. Then we . . .'

'. . . went to Tavistock and played football, then to Powder Mills. Tavistock was great and Powder Mills was boring . . .'

I wish Tom would stop interrupting, thought Jessica.

'You went in your London taxi-cab, sir,' put in the sergeant, eyes darting about the room. He scares me, thought Jessica, but we've done nothing wrong.

'Yes, I own it. It's my livelihood. The taxi's big enough for all of us and it's very reliable. Why do you ask?'

'It was noticed in Princetown today – you don't often get London taxi-cabs there, sir.'

'Well, it's fully licensed and insured and everything. You can check if you want to.'

'Well, sir,' said the older policeman, 'by an amazing coincidence, on the day and at the time you chose to visit Princetown these two prisoners escaped.'

'But we don't know anything about that!' burst out Tom.

'No, it's nothing to do with us,' added his father.

'I see you have a mixed family, sir,' Sergeant Skinner said, in a voice as sharp as his eyes.

'So?'

'Just interesting, sir.'

'If you think we've been helping convicts to escape driving round Dartmoor in a TAXI with us lot inside it, you must be joking . . .'

'Tom, be quiet,' shouted his father.

'. . . we'd stick out like a sore thumb. All the time. I get sick of it!'

'Only inquiring. We have to check everything, you see. Is this your cottage? Is there anyone else here, sir?'

'Yes, my brother, Peter Fraser. He's just gone to bed.'

'To bed. At this time of the evening? Is he ill?'

'No, but he's been playing at gigs in Cornwall, just driven back and he was very tired so he went up to have a rest.'

'Mmm,' said Sergeant Skinner.

'I know Peter,' said P.C. Mudge. 'He's played at some of our functions. And at the prison itself at certain times.'

'Has he now? He would have had contact with the prisoners then?' The sergeant smiled thinly.

I don't believe this, thought Jessica. Neither could Tom.

'Uncle Pete's got nothing to do with it! Hadn't you better be stopping *them* get away, instead of suspecting us? I mean, *he* wouldn't be much use helping convicts escape, would he?' he burst out, pointing at Jack, now fast asleep on Jessica.

'It would be a good idea if you didn't have quite so much to say, young fellow. It could get you into trouble one day. He's quiet now, isn't he?' The sergeant indicated Felix, sitting totally still and silent.

'Of course he is. He never says anything useful, anyway.'

'Tom!' everybody shouted, except Felix who grinned like mad. Why, he's OK, thought Jessica suddenly, and he's got more sense than Tom.

'We're going to search the premises now. I expect *you* can help us,' Sergeant Skinner said to Tom.

'What do these men look like?' Clem asked.

'One's fair-haired, with blue eyes, ordinary-looking, not very big but strong, clever and dangerous. Fast on his feet. Don't approach him. The other's big, dark-haired with a tattoo, "Mother", on his hand. He's slower and not so clever but can be trouble. They're involved with drugs and armed robbery and are known to be violent. I'll say again – especially to you, young man – don't go near them if you see them, but inform us. We'll check your house and garden, then, if it's all OK, you lock up when we've gone and stay inside.'

'There was something,' Jessica said, surprising even herself.

'What? Tell us. Where?'

Her dad broke in impatiently. 'Oh, you and Tom. You can't keep quiet, can you? Either of you. She's always imagining things.'

But Jessica continued. 'We stopped at Powder Mills on the way home and Dad and the boys were in the car, and Clem and Jack and me, we stood by the little bridge and then the cannon and they went back to the car but I saw a gully then, hidden with gorse and bushes and stuff and there was something – someone in that gully, I'm sure . . .'

'What?'

'I dunno. A shadow – it was too big for an animal. I was thinking about the Hairy Hands so I ran back to the car when Dad called.'

'The Hairy Hands?' asked Sergeant Skinner. 'What are they?'

'Just an old tale,' answered P.C. Mudge. 'You wouldn't know, being new here. Nothing to do with escaped convicts.'

The policemen searched the house, the caravan and the garden. Nothing. Pete slept on, and they would leave him for now, they said. At last they left, leaving the Pattersons and Frasers together, full of strange thoughts, and feeling terrible.

Chapter Eighteen

The moor must be crawling with police and wardens, and then the helicopters, the cars, the road-blocks, thought Jessica. And the dogs – the idea of the dogs scared her most of all. Imagine being hunted by a dog! She shivered, though the fire was burning brightly. They all sat, not wanting to go to bed, with the radio on, listening in case any news came through. Outside, the night was dark and still. Jessica kept looking at the clock but time had slowed down. Jack slept peacefully, sprawled half on her, half on the sofa, one hand clutching hers. She didn't dare move.

At last Pete came downstairs, still pale but OK, and made himself a huge mug of coffee.

'Sorry about that. I was just completely done in.'

'Tell us what happened. What made you run into something? Was it really the hands?' Jessica whispered, eyes nearly standing out of her head, gripping her plait with the hand that Jack wasn't holding.

'The police have been here while you were in bed,' Tom said, not in the least interested in Pete's story, only in his own.

'Police! What for? Surely not about the car?'

'No, no, not about your old banger,' answered Andrew. 'No, not that. There's two escaped prisoners on the run.'

'They suspected *us* of helping them!' cried Tom.

'No, they didn't,' snapped his father. 'They were just questioning us and searching everywhere in the neighbourhood. Just routine, I expect, Tom.'

'They looked in the shed and everywhere,' put in Felix, shaken out of his usual cool. 'And they said we were to stay inside until they'd caught them because these two were dangerous.'

'What were their names?' asked Pete.

'I don't know – I can't remember. But I think they'll be back later to question you this time.'

'Why didn't you wake me up?'

'You were too soundly asleep.'

'Oh, Pete – tell us what happened to you. Tell me – tell me about the hands . . .' said Jessica.

Her father groaned.

'Well – I was tired out,' Pete said. 'I'd hardly

slept. Once I almost nodded off. That shook me and I decided to stop for a while and rest, but I was nearly home and I came along that road, you know . . .'

'We know,' Jessica said.

'And it was the same. The car swerved. I was terrified. Something, not me, was driving the car, trying to kill me!'

'Was it the hands? Did you see them?' cried Jessica.

'I saw something – blurred, through a mist. Oh, I don't want to talk about it. I've never been so scared in the whole of my life. I can't drive as well as you, Andy, and . . .'

'You hit the wall and bashed the side of your car in,' Tom finished for him.

They all shivered, staring at one another. Clem got up and put some more logs on the fire and they drew nearer together – in their fear of the terrors outside they were almost united. Jessica dozed off, though she'd thought she'd never sleep again. It was almost midnight when she woke, her father shaking her.

'Jessica! Wake up! They've caught one of them and they think the other's got past the road-blocks and is on his way to London. It came over on local radio. I think you can go to bed now. We're OK.'

Clem lifted Jack, who didn't stir, and started heading up the stairs. Jessica followed, stumbling, half-asleep. Funny, she'd been dreaming about something, what was it? Whatever it was, it was not surprising with all that was happening. Yet, yet it wasn't about escaped prisoners or malevolent beings, it was something else.

She shook her head to clear it. None of it matters, she thought. I'll be in my own bed in my own bedroom tomorrow night. But for how long? Would Dad make them all move? Something stirred again – a memory, no, she couldn't place it – and she felt very sleepy. Home – home.

Chapter Nineteen

But they didn't go home after all. For the
next day turned out to be a glorious,
sunshiny, blue-skyey, as-fresh-as-new-
paint day. And Pete begged them to stay just a
while longer. He'd bought some fireworks
earlier and hoped they could let them off in the
garden even if it wasn't actually November the
fifth.

In the bright morning he seemed his usual
cheery self and they were all in good spirits
– convicts, ghosts, quarrels, problems were far
away. Who cared about them?

'You can get packed and ready tomorrow in
comfort,' said Pete. 'Today we'll light a fire,
bake potatoes and chestnuts . . . "Chestnuts
roasting on an open fire,"' he warbled. 'It'll be
fantastic . . .'

He found some old clothes (nobody had more
old clothes than Pete), and they made a Guy

Fawkes, with Clem in charge. A stuffed cushion for a head, a bobble hat, eyes, nose and mouth painted on, an old pipe of Pete's stuck in the raggedy mouth – yellow sweater, old jeans and boots completed him. They sat him on the kindling and logs that Pete and Andrew had been gathering, added to a fine collection of old rubbish that Pete had accumulated at one time or another.

Jessica put food ready in the kitchen, with Jack helping, or trying to.

'Happy Families, Jack,' she said to him.

'What, Jessica? What you say?'

'Nothing at all,' she laughed.

Andrew got them together to deliver a long lecture on being sensible with the fire and with the fireworks, especially Tom.

'Don't always pick on me, Dad,' he groaned. 'Be fair.'

'You are hard on him, you know,' said Clem. 'Tom's OK really. You should learn to trust him more.'

Andrew looked at her surprised, for Clem hardly ever criticized anyone, least of all him. He opened his mouth in reply, then closed it again. He wasn't annoyed. Everyone was in a good mood, waiting for the dark so that they could begin the celebrations.

'I shall burst all over the place,' cried Jack.

'Don't,' Jessica said. 'Think of the mess.'

They held hands and jumped up and down, as much as Jack could jump.

> 'From ghoulies and ghosties,
> Long leggity beasties,
> And things that go BUMP in the night,
> Especially escaped prisoners,
> Good Lord deliver us and send us
> Plenty of BANGS!'

sang Jessica.

It was a super, fantastic evening. The rockets, the Catherine Wheels, the Jumping Jacks all went off magnificently – no failures. The fire blazed up straight away, lighting up the dark but starry night, burning the guy until it fell into the red hot glow at the bottom of the fire, flaming away while they cheered and shouted and clapped. They ate their potatoes and sausages and chestnuts outside and at last, full and happy, even Tom, they turned to go into the house, laughing and talking.

'Where's Jack?' cried Clem, looking round, hand on the latch.

'He's with you,' cried Felix, straggling at the back.

'No, he isn't,' she replied. 'He's with you.'

'No . . .'

Jack was with no one.

'Jack, Jack,' they called. 'Come on, it's supper time now, you don't have to go to bed yet, come on, come on! Where are you? Where have you got to? Come on, don't mess about, you'll get cold! Jack, Jack, where are you now . . . ?'

'Tom, Felix – go search for him . . .'

'Oh, he'll come in a minute . . .'

'It's not like him, though. Not like . . .'

'Jack, Jack . . .'

They went through into the kitchen and followed through into the living-room.

A fair-haired man stood there, one arm holding Jack, the hand over his mouth, the other hand holding a knife to Jack's thin little neck. Jack's eyes were huge pools of fear and pain, for his twisted leg with its poor foot was trailing awkwardly on the floor. Jessica's stomach jolted and dropped into a freefall of terror.

They all stood frozen, staring, staring, except for Tom yelling, 'Don't you dare hurt him! Let him go!'

The man just stared at him icily. When he spoke his voice was low, unhurried.

'But I don't want to hurt this little chap. He's done nothing to me and I'll do nothing to him if you're sensible and do as you're told quickly and quietly. You two men go down into the cellar. Yes, I know it's there – I explored when you were all having fun outside. It's got a thick door with a key and no window. You two, go down there and you . . .' he nodded to Clem, '. . . lock the door securely.'

Andrew twitched angrily. Pete's eyes went over the room as if seeking a way out of all this. The man grew impatient.

'Move,' he snapped.

Slowly, looking helplessly at Jack, they went towards the cellar door under the stairs.

'Jess, Tom . . .' began Andrew, but the man's knife moved a little and they opened the door and stood at the top of the dark steps.

'Now, lock it,' he told Clem. She locked the door.

They could hear footsteps on the other side of the door and a terrible cry of, 'Clem, I'm sorry.' Tears ran down her face then, and Jessica put her arms round her.

'You beast,' yelled Tom. Felix's face was a mask. He took a step forward.

'Don't even think of it,' the man murmured quite gently, and Jack's leg jerked spasmodically. The boys sank back.

'Now,' he went on. 'We're going to do this nice and quickly.' Still holding Jack, he motioned them out of the door and towards the taxi-cab.

'Hurry it. I can't hang about, you know. GET IN!' he snarled suddenly.

Slowly the boys and Jessica piled into the back. Tom was silent now, but Jessica knew what an effort it was costing him – she could sense him almost exploding. She felt rigid and almost paralysed with fear.

'I'll hit you from here,' Tom spat out suddenly. 'Me and Felix will.'

'Then I'll hurt this little fellow.'

Clem turned on the headlights and bolts of light cut the darkness. She turned the engine on and pressed the throttle. The taxi misfired once, then started up jerkily and screeched along the drive.

'Drive properly,' he said. 'I'm sure you can drive very well.'

'But what's the point?' asked Felix as they went along. 'You can't get away in this.'

'We stick out like a sore thumb,' Tom said, as he had once before.

'That's just the point. Your taxi-cab's been seen round here, and your mixed family. If anyone sees us, I'm your dad. I saw you at Powder Mills and thought then what a splendid escape vehicle it would be. The police think I'm heading for London, but a mate is waiting at a tiny little hidden Cornish cove with a boat for Europe. You, this happy family . . .'

Oh, no, screamed Jessica inside.

'. . . are carrying on with your holiday into Cornwall. I'll let you go there if you're well-behaved and if you're lucky. Otherwise I'll drop you in the harbour! Get going. It's not too far.'

Chapter Twenty

It came to Jessica that all her life had been
leading up to this, that everything up till
now had been learning time ready for this
exam, as if the awful, dreaded day had arrived
at last when she would be tested by the monster
man who sat near, holding Jack so cruelly. She
was once more between Tom and Felix, shivering as they drove through the night, following
the car headlights that cut through the mist.
She grabbed the boys' hands but they pulled
away. They were tense, alert.

'I want to be ready to attack!' Tom hissed.

'Shut up – you at the back!'

They all subsided on to the seat. Hopelessness
crawled over Jessica, numbing her limbs, weak-
ening her will-power. What *could* they do? How
could they save Jack? And themselves? Again
the hopeless feeling like poison in her veins, rot
in her bones. She must believe that this man

could be beaten, that they could escape from this nightmare they were caught in. She clutched at little indications of hope.

The boys were glinting at each other, eyes bright, feet, hands ready to do something, anything, giving the tiniest, slightest nod to each other as if planning a football manoeuvre in some vital game. To Jessica they seemed, for a moment, identical, interchangeable, one black, one white, Tom–Felix/Felix–Tom, aspects of the same thing. Surely they could – could they? She was sure they were about to spring together – now!

'If either of you two move I'll cut off the tip of his ear. It won't really hurt – but it'll BLEED!'

She could hear Jack's little choking sob of terror, she could feel the tears running down his cheeks. The eyes of the boys beside her glazed over with the same hopelessness that she felt sweeping over her. Perhaps . . . perhaps at the end of the journey, when the car stopped, perhaps – perhaps they could rush him then, overwhelm him with the force of numbers.

By now Dad and Pete should have found a way out. Surely they would get themselves out of the cellar and be calling for help, for the police. Get to the police quickly! Oh, save us, Dad!

A car was approaching. Hope stirred. Clem drove on, a living statue behind the wheel. Could they somehow stop this car?

'Dip the lights properly,' the man snapped. 'No funny stuff.'

The car drove on and hope died again. Seated in the middle, Jessica could just make out the cats'-eyes winking at them, drawing them along the dark, lonely, lonely road.

Something flew almost into the windscreen, swooping aside at the very last minute. Was it a bird? A bat? Some creature out of a nightmare? No, the nightmare creature was in the cab with them, holding the point of a knife at Jack, the gentlest, funniest lad, now silent and terrified. Jessica could feel that fear even stronger than her own as they drove on and on, with Jack a hostage, all of them hostages.

This holiday was doomed, she thought, right from the start. If we'd gone home today we'd have missed this horror, we could have been back safely in our house, with its picture of Mum smiling on the landing above the stairs. Help us, Mum, help save us. Look after your children, Tom and me, but not just Tom and me, me and Tom but Clem and Jack and Felix as well, for we're all in it together. We are together now. Probably for always, for we can't ever forget this. Happy Families United Team. You won't mind us being together if we ever escape from this nightmare. Help us – please – all of us. I know I thought you'd resent them and I fought for us, against Clem, and I was wrong. I specially didn't want Clem, so I vandalized things and I'm so sorry – and Tom got the blame, not me, not *good* Jessica who was really *bad* Jessica because she hated them all, because they took *my* place with Dad and were going to take our place with you.

Please forgive me and save us all – for they somehow are our family now and I don't want us all to be here in danger with this man who's hurting Jack . . .

HELP . . . please help.

Tom rubbed over the misty window with his sleeve. It was clearer here, and Jessica, looking out of her prayers and her misery, saw . . .

. . . a flat bleak road, a grass verge, a ditch, a grey granite wall, behind it the black trees.

The car swerved.

Clem gasped, 'I can't hold it.'

The man yelled, 'Don't play me up!'

The car swerved, skidded, turning towards the wall and the ditch. The man, holding Jack with his legs, reached over to grab the steering-wheel to control and turn it to safety.

But huge muscular hands – with black hairs on them – fastened over his hands and Jessica saw them clearly as the taxi sped towards the wall and she spun off into the dark.

Epilogue

Those whose history we followed can be found again eighteen months later.

It's a clear sunny spring day and through the open French windows, leading on to a large garden lawn, shouts of, 'Yes, now, take that, great, leave it, shoot, brilliant, fantastic, here, watch it, RUBBISH,' are coming from two boys – no, three – playing football. Two of them are large and strong and they're making allowances for the third, who's much smaller with a bit of a limp, but they're doing it very skilfully so he doesn't realize this.

At a desk in the far corner of the biggish room sits a man marking piles of exercise books. It's Andrew Fraser, who has returned to teaching. He says after what they all went through he can cope with anything (even school) now.

On a comfortable sofa sits a girl with hair

flowing down her back. She bounces a baby up and down and he reaches out for a strand of the bright hair and gurgles.

'You would have to be a boy, wouldn't you? Who'd have thought I'd end up with four brothers, Billy Fraser! Come on, it's time to meet your mum from work.'

She carries him upstairs to change him, pausing briefly on the way to say 'Hi!' and for him to wave his small fist at the two portraits on the landing, both painted by her father, of her mother and her stepmother, Clem.

Far away on Dartmoor, Peter Fraser, just about to embark on an American tour, leaves flowers for a prison grave.

'Why?' he is asked.

'He was lost, wicked and unhappy but somehow he brought happiness to others,' he smiles. 'In fact two *bad* things – a convict and a ghost – made a very good one: a happy family.'

And Pete goes singing on his way, wearing one ear-ring and a particularly hideous hand-knitted (by him) bobble hat.

Acknowledgements

The author extends a personal thank you to Terry Bound of Exeter for the story of Carlo at Powder Mills on pages 86–7.

The extract from 'Tom Bone' by Charles Causley on page 58 is reprinted from *Collected Poems* by permission of David Higham Associates Ltd.

The Turbulent Term of Tyke Tiler

by Gene Kemp

Tyke Tiler is very fond of jokes – that's why there are so many in this story. And Tyke is also fond of Danny Price, who is not too bright and depends a lot on his friend. In fact, medium-bright Tyke and medium-dim Danny add up to double trouble, especially during their last term at Cricklepit Combined School.

Gowie Corby Plays Chicken

by Gene Kemp

Gowie Corby is the terror of Cricklepit
Combined School. He's mean, and he
wants no help and no friends – apart from
Boris Karloff, his pet rat. So when an
ancient cellar is uncovered at the school,
with ghosts and all, nothing is surely
going to prevent him from spending a
night there. Especially when he'll be called
chicken if he doesn't.

Charlie Lewis Plays for Time

by Gene Kemp

For Charlie Lewis and his friends in class 4M, the last term of Cricklepit Combined School *could* have been fun. That is, if the beloved Mr Merchant hadn't broken several bones in the holidays and been replaced by the unbearable Mr Carter (alias Garters). As it is, they've just got to make the best of it – a difficult task for the dynamic Trish Moffat and her lovable but eccentric twin brother, Rocket, who's always getting into trouble; and worse still for quiet, unassuming Charlie, whose famous mother just happens to be Mr Carter's favourite concert pianist …

Zowey Corby
and the
Black Cat Tunnel

by Gene Kemp

Lucy said at last, 'I'm sad because I don't want to be here at this rotten school and I wish I was dead.'

Zowey Corby isn't sure she's going to like 'Posh Git' Lucy Ledley-Brown. Lucy is the new girl in Zowey's class at Cricklepit Combined School, but she definitely doesn't want to be there. Everything seems so strange to Lucy – especially Tiro and his friend Hopper. But just about everyone is scared of Tiro; and not many people would like Hopper for a friend – certainly not Lucy. So when Hopper falls hopelessly in love with her, that just adds to her problems …

Jason Bodger and the Priory Ghost

by Gene Kemp

When Jason Bodger, school menace and
student teacher's nightmare, visits a priory
with Class 4Z, he has a most peculiar and
disturbing experience. He sees a strange
girl walking towards him high up on a
non-existent beam. Mathilda de
Chetwynde, born in a castle over 700 years
ago, has decided that Jason is just the
person she's been waiting for – and there's
not a thing Jason can do about it! A
hilarious, riotous tale in which the
twentieth century meets the Middle Ages!

READ MORE IN PUFFIN

For children of all ages, Puffin represents quality and variety – the very best in publishing today around the world.

For complete information about books available from Puffin – and Penguin – and how to order them, contact us at the appropriate address below. Please note that for copyright reasons the selection of books varies from country to country.

On the worldwide web: www.penguin.com, for links to Penguin companies worldwide.

In the United Kingdom: Please write to *Dept. EP, Penguin Books Ltd, Bath Road, Harmondsworth, West Drayton, Middlesex UB7 0DA*

In the United States: Please write to *Consumer Sales, Penguin USA, P.O. Box 999, Dept. 17109, Bergenfield, New Jersey 07621-0120.* VISA and MasterCard holders call 1-800-253-6476 to order Penguin titles

In Canada: Please write to *Penguin Books Canada Ltd, 10 Alcorn Avenue, Suite 300, Toronto, Ontario M4V 3B2*

In Australia: Please write to *Penguin Books Australia Ltd, P.O. Box 257, Ringwood, Victoria 3134*

In New Zealand: Please write to *Penguin Books (NZ) Ltd, Private Bag 102902, North Shore Mail Centre, Auckland 10*

In India: Please write to *Penguin Books India Pvt Ltd, 706 Eros Apartments, 56 Nehru Place, New Delhi 110 019*

In the Netherlands: Please write to *Penguin Books Netherlands bv, Postbus 3507, NL-1001 AH Amsterdam*

In Germany: Please write to *Penguin Books Deutschland GmbH, Metzlerstrasse 26, 60594 Frankfurt am Main*

In Spain: Please write to *Penguin Books S. A., Bravo Murillo 19, 1° B, 28015 Madrid*

In Italy: Please write to *Penguin Italia s.r.l., Via Felice Casati 20, I–20124 Milano*

In France: Please write to *Penguin France S. A., 17 rue Lejeune, F–31000 Toulouse*

In Japan: Please write to *Penguin Books Japan, Ishikiribashi Building, 2–5–4, Suido, Bunkyo-ku, Tokyo 112*

In South Africa: Please write to *Longman Penguin Southern Africa (Pty) Ltd, Private Bag X08, Bertsham 2013*